Have you heard? It's in the stars

Maud's Memoirs

EDITED BY

Sally Warrington

"Maud speaks to our inner fish"

–PAUL SINCLAIR, FACE OF '68

"Inspiring…"

–POPE FRANCIS, HOLY FATHER,
AND FORMER WALTHAMSTOW RESIDENT

"A complete revelation"

–MONIQUE HART, CELEBRITY CHEF

"A person of Interest"

–FEDERAL INTELLIGENCE SERVICE, GERMANY

"A person of Interest"

–MI5, UK

"A determined, challenging creature"

–APOLLO LUNT, BOOKER PRIZE WINNER 1993

"Nice ass for an old broad"

–CHUCK O'HARA, FORMER WHITE HOUSE CHIEF STRATEGIST

"Simply unbelievable…"

–ELECTRA VAUGHAN, FASHION DESIGNER, AND 20TH CENTURY ICON

For Kitty

Contents

Foreword

Legendary is an adjective bandied around all too often these days, and yet how difficult it is to have the name – Maud Jollybottom – in a sentence without using that term. Starting out as a junior reporter in the swinging 1960s, progressing into the worlds of fashion and popular music in the 1970s and 80s, Maud developed her special gifts in astrological counselling to become the confidante of artists, politicians, and celebrities. These memoirs have been compiled to illustrate the phenomenal climb of Maud's rise to fame, from the Old Rectory in her beloved Clenching, to the Buckingham Palace VIP invitation list. During her time as a celestial advisor, she has counselled Hollywood stars on their planetary challenges and has illuminated British society – with a brief, recent foray in the US – on how to read the planets to our advantage, understand the inner potential we all carry, and how to embrace life and all it has, in Maud's words, to offer us. Beloved by radio, television and all other forms of modern media, Maud has been the voice of the oracle throughout the decades. This work hopes to capture the essence of Maud on her special journey into our hearts and help us, as ordinary mortals, appreciate her very special skills and talents.

Introduction

2018

The idea for this book came to me when, after a few years away from the media glare, the name Maud Jollybottom was mentioned during a Radio 4 programme. The programme's subject matter, interestingly, was about cold war espionage in the 1980s, an unlikely context in which, I thought, the celebrity astrologer would feature. As I listened to the programme, however, I became increasingly interested – her involvement in so many situations was intriguing. Eventually I began to read and research extensively anything about the mysterious Maud and her career. Although more generally known as a celebrity astrologer, famous for her pithy, some may say offensive astrological assessments – there were rumours of international spying in her background, as well as Eurovision commentating, hostage negotiation, US presidential connections and now, in her senior years, whispers of a Special Envoy to the UN role. Was there any public role she wasn't prepared to undertake, and succeed at? I realised, up to now, no one has got to the heart of Maud. Who really was this legendary creature? Where did she come from, and more importantly, how had she got here?

I felt compelled to put together a biography of sorts which would include some of her astrological press cuttings, and I wanted her input and hopefully, her blessing. I knew she had always kept journals, so I wrote to her, asking her permission for access to these. Eventually Maud agreed to my seeing edited versions, but wanting a more rounded view of her life, I sought further background information from her inner circle. I felt it was important to include contributions from those who had known her early in her career. It was a surprise to discover that the celebrated fashion designer, Electra Vaughan, a childhood companion of Maud, had excerpts from Maud's journals in her possession. I'm still not entirely sure how this came about, and both Maud and Electra remain tight-lipped on the subject. Maud, until recently resisted any kind of modern communication method such as email, and instead preferred to utilise her dog who responded in barking code when asked simple questions. This was understandably limiting to interviewers, and previous attempts at a biography had faltered over the dog basket. However, the kindly Electra Vaughan offered to supply an account of Maud's early history in Clenching, as supplied verbally by her mother, Doris Vaughan, before she passed away. (Legal notice: as a verbatim account none of the details therein can be verified).

I wrote to Maud when I felt ready to publish, and she responded, tacitly, if not whole-heartedly, in agreement. At least, she told me the planets were harmonious to any new projects undertaken by Geminis, so I took that as a Yes. Clearly, she had also done her research on me. I showed her the final manuscript prior to publication, and although I still await her blessing I remain, so far, unscathed from physical attack, from Maud or her family, so I will have to be content with that.

These days Maud lives a quiet life, away from the spotlight. Instead, she prefers the solitude of her garden at the Old Rectory or isolating for days at a time in her custom-built isolation tank vessel,[1] moored nearby. The loss of her most recent *Shi Tzu*, Moseley VII, was a great blow and Maud rarely made an appearance without him. I was delighted when my agent told me there was media interest in making a documentary about Maud, based on this book. It seems Maud Jollybottom, conveyor of wisdom "*From the Planets to the Stars*"[2], is still a fascinating and enigmatic subject to her fans and will continue to be so for many years to come. She

---

[1] Maud's Isolation Tank was custom built and designed by her former client, ex rock-God Paul Sinclair.

[2] "*From the Planets to the Stars*" is the title of Maud's 2018 self-help book featuring interviews and readings with various celebrities. Published by Clenchings, a subsidiary of Jollybottom Publications, Inc. Available at all good bookshops and a few not so good ones.

may even leave the Rectory, or the tank, to appear at her own premiere — let's hope we are favoured on such a special occasion.

Finally, in writing this introduction, I thought it would be sensible to include one of many cuttings from Maud's ground-breaking website, *Jolly Stars*. Cuttings from the website and from a variety of other sources follow each of her twelve adventures through the zodiac. The excerpt below is from the *Jolly Stars* series on Holidays, 2016, explaining which zodiac sign makes the best holiday partner, what sort of holiday to expect to share with them, and in some cases who should be avoided, on a holiday or in everyday life. Read and enjoy!

From Holidays with Maud ...

Summer has at long last arrived. The days are filled with sunlight, and the long summer evenings bring even this sleepy village out of hibernation. The lanes and hedges are alive with the sound of busy Clenchers. I prefer to "*holiday*", a term my dear friend Somerset (Maugham) used to tease me about, in the South of France, out of season. I like my little dogs to accompany me to Nice, where we often enjoy an early morning stroll along *La Promenade des Anglaise*. The French are much more open minded towards our little furry friends than the English. In France no-one bats an eyelid if I take a little Shih Tzu on the beach!

And now, dear friends, to my astrological observations. Everyone has their own likes and dislikes when it comes to "*holidaying*", and it is my duty to highlight areas and activities each zodiacal sign will find fulfilling. I'm going to break with tradition this time – the signs will not be listed in astrological order, rather in a descending level of popularity. Let me explain this further for those less able amongst us. We will start with Pisces – a sign peopled by the moderately pleasant if a little unstable, and end with Scorpio, always slightly repellent on some level. Forgive me if I'm rather sporadic in providing these bulletins – my astrological messages are often a wearisome burden to discharge, especially from someone as delicate as myself. In some cases, it may be sensible to revisit this site later in the year. If you are by nature slow, as in Sagittarius, it probably doesn't matter as you won't be able to grasp it anyway.

Cruel, but fair has always been Maud's motto. Happy summer holidays everyone. See you at the Autumnal Equinox with exciting news of the late September Blood Moon!

Jolly Astrolly! website, August 2015

CHAPTER 1

Aquarius

Clenching, 1941

(As recalled verbatim by Doris Vaughan)

"… well, Maud's father, he was christened Ganglion[1], but they always called him "Dodger" because of how he got fired out of a cannon, or had them knives thrown at 'im, as part of his act, see? He never hurt himself, so he "dodged" it, every time. Of course, them in the village called him "Dodger" because it was wartime, and somehow – no-one knew how, exactly – he'd managed to avoid being called up on account of his flat feet, or something … You might have known a Jollybottom, a *Slidey Arse*, as we called 'em, would've have got out of it … for a while, anyway.

Anyway, he first came back in about 1941, with his new missus. She was expecting Maud. The pair of 'em had been working in music hall and circus and what not – she was an acrobat when she first met 'im and they did turns together in shows and the like … she was always very highly strung, in more ways than one … one of the *Jumping Jehoshaphats*! They

---

[1]   Grandfather Jolyon Jollybottom liked to give his children names with a medical slant. Hence Ganglion's twin sisters, who arrived in 1925, and who he called Flipper and Rosy, were in reality Fallopia and Rosacea.

were a high wire turn. See, she was Jericho, there were seven sisters and they all had names from the bible … Well, when the war came that life sort of ended for 'em, due to the bombing and that, so he came home, tail between his legs, looking for shelter, like. He'd fallen out with his father, Old Man Jollybottom, when he was a young 'un and ran away to join the circus. During the war though, with men gone overseas, he was needed in the family firm, so he walked straight back into a job with his father's blessing, and with plenty of room for a family at the Old Rectory. Typical *Slidey Arse* …

Jericho, she never settled, though … her life had been exciting and travellin' round the country, and that – not quiet like, living in a little village and not mixing much with anyone. It was boring 'ere for her, being a stranger like and we had the black out – her sisters couldn't visit cos of the petrol being rationed, so no buses either. I think it sent her funny in the 'ed and 'e didn't have much patience for it. Sometimes 'e kept her locked up when she had one of her cryin' spells and that … only in her room not in a cupboard or nothin' – just until she calmed down. She used to do her acrobat exercises and that while she was locked in. We could hear her jumpin' around and her somersaultin' – I 'spose it was all she had to do once the babies were being minded or 'havin their nap. She must have rehearsed her escape for when the time was right. She knew how to get out of that rectory handcuffed and blindfolded – it was the turn she used to do, see with 'er sisters? Second nature it came like … She climbed up on the roof one day and catapulted herself somehow – and she was 'off, over the fields and away to who knows where … 'they never heard from 'er, again. Mind you, she did leave that little Maud and her sister behind. Can't say that was good for either of them … funny little kids they were, I were sorry for them. That Maud could be a little madam, but she always looked after her little sister and brother. The family never really knew where Jericho had gone, so Dodger told the little 'uns she had gone off to the moon and the stars. She was an acrobat see – she'd gone flying up in the clouds. I never knew where she went, but there was a war on, so we just had to take it in our stride … He was too strict with his ways was Dodger, but 'e was a charmer and 'e was dashing, like a film star. Just like Clark Gable …

Anyways, he carries on working in the family printing … and has big ideas about modernising the firm. He wants to modernise it, does Dodger, but the Old Man's dead set against it. But Dodger, maybe with a little help from his pals in the Masons, gets a shiny, new printing machine – the talk of the county, he says. Well, they only had 'ole boys working there – the youngsters had been called up, see – they had to learn it, it was all new to 'em. Dodger says the firm won't have a need for men when all the machines are new, like his one. The Old Man don't like it but he's not the same since the war started. He could remember the last one too clearly.

We all keep on carrying on till one day this big, black police car turns up at the Rectory and two men, one in an overcoat and a trilby and the other a copper in uniform, ask to speak to Dodger. Old Jimmy, the gardener, he's working in the garden, tells 'em to go to the printing works to find Dodger. The next thing we know is the Old Man's had a funny turn at the works, and he's been brought 'ome. Not by Dodger though, he's gone missing. The works has had some sort of order slapped on it, and closed down, while some investigation takes place. Well later, hours later, it looks likely that Dodger has been using his nice new machinery to print off ration book coupons, on the quiet, like. Doing his bit, see for the war effort. His personal war effort. Dodger being dodgy.

No one knows where he's gone, but as luck would have it – if you can call it luck – four days later the printing works is bombed to bits by the German planes on their way to Gloucester. Everything was destroyed. Including Dodger's nice new machinery. No one got hurt 'cos it was night time, but there still weren't no word from Dodger. We all carried on and pitched in with the children and the house. A few months later the Old Man got a letter from Dodger sayin' he'd joined up, in London, he couldn't say where he was now but to give his love to the children.

Well, he never saw them again till after the war was over. He just turns up one day, bold as brass, and walks in through the front gate like he'd just been out for a stroll. It was a hot day in 1946 – I'll never forget it. He used his front door key and walked straight through to the kitchen where I'm getting the tea ready. *"Hello Doris"* he said. He looked so handsome in his suit, I felt my heart flip over, as if he had been my husband, and not

Jericho's. "*Have you missed me?*" He was always a wrong 'un, that Dodger, but a right charmer, too …

Aquarius Sun Sign cuttings

Holidays with Aquarius

Developments in science and cosmology are always of interest to Aquarians. Out-of-this-world exploration always appeals to the sign challenged by maintaining relationships of any kind with creatures on this planet. The idea of a perfect Aquarian holiday therefore is a punishing 10-year training programme in a North Korean space camp. Aquarians abroad are fascinated by the ways and cultures of others, so long as it's made clear they're visiting and not seeking asylum. They do like to travel often however so just keep in mind their overwhelming selfishness and have their bag packed, ready for their exit! If you must tag along don't expect any sort of attention or interest from them whatsoever and you won't go wrong on your happy holiday together.

Blue Yonder Travel Magazine, 2017

Your Aquarian Date

Let's start at the very beginning. No one could ever say an Aquarian isn't a friendly soul. Male or female or any fashionable modern variant, Aquarius is always the sociable one at the office do who will find you a drink, draw you out of yourself, and turn on a dazzling, welcoming smile. It's very, very easy to warm to one, especially when they have such an interesting turn of conversation, and obviously find you fascinating. And they *will* find you fascinating, for a brief, shiny moment, so make the most of it, because you will have your work cut out keeping him interested in a second longer than necessary.

Is He Into You? website, January 2006

MUSICAL AQUARIUS

Although you have the reputation of being the most selfish sign in the zodiac, many of the recent snarl-ups have not been your fault. Under the sign of the Water Bearer, Mercury in retrograde has been up to all sorts of mischief. Performance dates that suddenly changed and rehearsals cancelled – best to put that terrifying multi-date contract in a locked drawer until September is a distant memory. Benevolent Jupiter, however, is on your side Aquarius, which is more than fortunate as few others are. Although your innovation and curiosity lead musically where others follow, your sheer bloody self-importance often dictates you tread a lonely pathway. Try keeping time with the boys in the band in future, as 2018 indicates all your secret shenanigans, and there have been plenty this year, will be revealed to the world, causing any supporting players to slip away.

Riffin' with Maud, From The Riff Magazine, September 2017

Sporty Aquarius

You are drawn to any extreme, dare-devil type of sporting activity, and relish a training programme that takes you away from the family for years at a time. You enjoy meeting new people and making friends with unknowns, viewing any change of direction as a challenge to be relished. Extreme snowboarding among the Laplanders, or snorg-boggling in Western Sahara is just your cup of tea, so take a family album with you. Don't forget to have the children write their names on their photos as it may be embarrassing if you don't recognise them at the airport when you finally return. They certainly won't have a clue who you are.

The Catholic Herald, Year of our Lord, 1995

♎

CHAPTER 2

Libra

Cliveden, 1961

The air was cooler out on the terrace, and I sat down at one of the small tables by the pool. The moon was cloud covered, but there were still tiny, twinkling fairy lights around the pool area, and discreet lighting spotted around the impressive lawns. I lit a Sobranie and fidgeted to sit comfortably on the wooden chair.

The vast house – more a palace, really, was sleeping – it was long past midnight – but I thought I could hear movement in some bushes to my right. A sudden loud giggle, and then, the blonde girl I'd seen earlier that day in the swimming pool appeared on the terrace. She looked like a young deer, startled at where she found herself. She was wearing a bath robe at least four sizes too big for her, with some monogrammed insignia on the breast pocket. She was barefoot and her blonde hair hung loose around her shoulders. She pulled a *"aren't I a naughty girl?"* face as if she was a small child, and then came and sat down at my table. The bathrobe fell open – I couldn't avoid staring with horror when it was clear she was completely naked underneath. She looked back at me insolently, uncaring.

"Give us one of your fags, doll?" she asked.

7

I offered her my packet and flicked my new lighter, a present from Grandpa.

"What did you say your name was again?" she asked. I picked up on a slight Welsh accent that had previously been hidden.

"Maud" I replied. *"And you are Mandy, I believe?"*

"That's right – you believe right" she said in a mocking way.

"Is someone with you?" I asked, gesturing at the bushes.

"Not likely, I've escaped for now – they'll stay out of sight if they know what's good for them".

She slowly exhaled smoke and examined me with her big, brown eyes.

"What about you – are you escaping someone?"

I wanted to say it's none of your business, you rude little hussy …

"No. I needed some air and thought this was a good spot".

"Where's your sister?" she asked.

"In bed". I was irritated by this girl and was *furious* with my sister. Krystal was in bed and entertaining someone she had only met that evening at dinner. Woken by their noisy fumbling in the room next door, I was reaching deeply for the essential *sang-froid* I was known for, out here in the dark.

"Where do you come from?" Mandy's chipper little voice broke into my thoughts.

"From a small town called Clenching. In the Cotswolds – I doubt you've heard of it. I doubt anyone's heard of it in the outside world".

"Clenching?" She laughed. *"CLENCHING?? That sounds uncomfortable". I come from Llanelli, but I live in London now. With Stephen."*

"What do you do there?" I asked, searching for the right words.

"Oh, a bit of modelling, making friends … " she giggled again.

I was intrigued by the idea of making friends as an occupation, and the way she said it made it sound unwholesome, somehow. Even if I felt a little nervous, I wanted to know more about her and her way of life in London. And how I could get there.

"Tell me more about yourself, Mandy."

People always love hearing this. They usually hesitate modestly, but I was learning how to coax information out of them, and by going down the astrology route, people gave surprisingly personal information away.

And I was already good at reading sun signs, at this stage of my career.

She giggled again. *"What would you like to know, doll?"*

"Erm, I know – when's your birthday?"

… and we were off. It was about an hour later when she stubbed the third or fourth cigarette out on the ground and got up to leave. I bade her a polite goodnight and watched her pad swiftly away through the bushes, pulling the robe around her tightly against the cold night air.

I hadn't taken Mandy and her friend Christine for the debutante type I'd come up against before, and my perception had been accurate. I'd made conversation in the polite way Krystal and I had been taught at finishing school and understood the two girls were staying in a cottage on the grounds with their male friend, Stephen. At first, I'd taken him to be an uncle perhaps, some sort of male relative anyway, but he turned out to have a chaperone role, surprisingly. Mandy had painted a rather different picture of Stephen.

We'd driven to Cliveden at the crack of dawn that day in a rather nifty little Austin Sprite, owned by Krystal's friend, Rupert Haut-Dougbreah (or Hot Dog-Breath as he was known at school). He was currently a law student and it seemed unlikely he would be joining the family business. The Hauts, as they were known, had been butchers for generations. The family name was shortened to Hauts for the convenience of signwriters among others, but they were proud of their Norman ancestry and obviously still practiced their bloodthirsty ways in the privacy of the Haut-Dougbreah abattoir. Rupert was older than Krystal and me, but his family had a good name in town and our parents had given their consent to our weekend away under his wing. The invitation had come from some rather highfalutin' friends of his parents who lived in Berks, overlooking the Thames. I look back and wonder now, how, and why Rupert was invited, and what exactly the connection was between the families, but it was all rather exciting then and people preferred to avoid looking at things too closely.

We'd been staggered at the scale of the house when we arrived. Even budding lawyer Rupert seemed struck dumb at the immense and magnificent stately pile, based in over 300 acres of beautiful Berkshire woodland. It looked like a baronial palace from a fairy tale. It certainly gave me much to think about in terms of Rupert's parents and their circle of acquaintances. Perhaps I should be a little more encouraging towards his friendship with my sister, although it looked more of a dance partnership rather than a romantic pairing. They'd won a few jiving competitions and spent most weekends in a dance hall somewhere. I was envious in a way. Krystal was so easily pleased with her small-town lot, whereas I craved excitement and independence. And that included leaving home, or de-Clenching, as soon as physically possible.

I was so pleased I'd checked the dress code beforehand. Both Krystal and I had included our little black dresses in case dinner turned out to be a formal matter. We were fortunate in knowing an excellent seamstress who went by the odd nickname of "Sparky"[1]. She was a village girl who helped mother with the cleaning, and who had an absolute gift for dressmaking. Krystal and I really appreciated her and made a point of giving her and her mother first refusal before giving our old clothes away to the church jumble. We always bought them little knicks knacks, or sticks of rock, from days out at the seaside. I know they were grateful to be remembered by us. And to have employment with us. They were poor people, obviously, but that must never stop one from being helpful, where one can be.

Anyway, I chose to wear my Little Black Dress (made up from a Vogue pattern spotted in Woolworths) with Grandma Jollybottom's pearls, and my hair looked rather nice – even if I say so – as I wore it brushed back from my face in the style of Princess Margaret Rose. It was such a pity the Princess didn't have someone like me to help and advise her – a quiet little thing in need of some confidence boosting from one blessed with insight into the troubled heart of a shy, retiring Leo. Recently married to a Taurus, heaven help them.

Krystal backcombed and pinned her long blonde hair into a bouffant to show off her inherited drop diamond earrings. Of course, neither Grandma's pearls nor Krystal's earrings were worth a ha'pence as we used to say in the old, pre-decimalised days, but we carried this off with the *je*

---

[1]   See chapter 10 for more on "Sparky", or Electra as she now prefers to be known

ne sais quoi the Jollybottom clan excelled in. "Appearance is everything" as Grandpa Jollybottom[2] strictly enforced.

Dinner at Cliveden was very grand. The room we had dined in was enormous and there were plenty of serving staff to look after us all. I was introduced for the first time to the gracious couple hosting the event, some distinguished guests (including a French and a Russian gentleman who helpfully spoke each other's language as well as impeccable English), some political folk, and the Harley Street chummy and his two young lady friends. There was also a TV quiz celebrity and a hit parade singer I'd never heard of, but who Krystal was thrilled to meet. Fortunately, my sister had been seated almost opposite to me, so I was able to gently prod her ankle with my stiletto if it looked like she was about to open her mouth and speak. This was done purely out of kindness – Krystal rarely said anything memorable but if by chance she did, people recalled her remarks for all the wrong reasons.

But I am wandering far away from 1961 and our attendance at this important, and what was to be, fateful society event. I noted the look of Krystal's disappointment when she realised Rupert was seated at the other end of the table. He looked happy enough, twittering away with his distinguished table neighbours. Krystal, on the other hand, listened impassively yet politely to the Russian gentleman at her side, her expression revealing nothing. I found this reassuring. He took care to make sure her wine glass was full, even though there were waiting staff hovering around the table. One of these, a tall, handsome young man, caught my eye as he effortlessly moved up and down the periphery. I remember

---

[2] Grandfather Jollybottom, like his son Ganglion, had also enjoyed a rather disreputable career as a music hall entertainer, before settling to a life in the Cotswold countryside. He did not, however qualify as a "confirmed Bachelor" having successfully knocked up various scullery and milkmaids in his time. During his theatrical career he managed to write some songs that were immensely popular and were whistled by delivery boys all over the empire, including:

"*Don't dangle over the mangle, Gertie!*" a big seller before WW1.

"*Larkin' in the darkin*" made famous by *Oopsa Wotnot* and his *Odelairs*, back in the day.

glancing down in Rupert's direction – it seemed he was watching the handsome footman as well.

For some reason I had the merest glimmer of intuition – as a psychic being I often do – and as I watched the footman move towards Rupert's place at the table, I wasn't surprised when he placed his hand on the footman's arm, as if to decline the food being served. It lingered on the arm just a fraction too long, as they exchanged a brief but telling glance between them. My sister seemed to be warming to the attention paid by the Russian gentleman beside her, and the free-flowing wine was obviously helping. At least she was acting happily enough, smiling in all the right places, and wiggling her bouffant hairdo at his jokes – I desperately hoped she and her hairdo stayed upright for the evening.

The meal eventually came to an end, and the men shuffled off somewhere to smoke cigars and drink brandy. The females gravitated towards the terrace for cigarettes and nightcaps – I had to explain to Krystal this wasn't an item to put on her head and she liked the idea once it made sense to her, but truthfully even I was a little overawed at the ladies we found ourselves mixing with, so we made our excuses and retired for the night. All the females were elegantly dressed and bejewelled but the two young ones, the girls called Mandy and Christine, were nowhere to be seen.

The rest of the weekend passed in a happy haze of hot weather and swimming pool fun. Although I was furious with Krystal's reckless behaviour, she acted discreetly over the next two days and did nothing to draw attention to herself. It turned out her night time gentleman caller was Russian, and little was seen of him over the following day. He made an appearance around lunchtime, and then vanished again for the rest of the day. The meal on Saturday evening was a more informal affair arranged buffet style in a beautiful anteroom to the pool, and the hosts had laid on two singers, with guitars, to entertain us in the evening. Once again, I noticed Rupert's rapport with the handsome footman as he bent to refill his glass – it was if they'd known each other for years.

We made our way back to Clenching around midday on the Sunday. Rupert had some family thing he needed to be back for, and the weather had become humid and uncomfortable. The car was hot and cramped with us and our luggage, and when the storm eventually broke, we all felt a bit out of sorts, seething with a brief but violent hatred of each other and sorry the glamorous weekend was over.

It was much later in 1963 the events of that weekend would come back to haunt me. Fortunately, and remembering these were pre-pill days, there had been no repercussions for Krystal. However, when the newspaper vultures in June of that year pounced and denounced the whole party set at Cliveden two years previous, I nervously waited for us to be included. I didn't want Krystal's liaison to become public – Russians were toxic in 1963 after the recent spy scandals. Although, in fairness, no one in their right mind could imagine Krystal working for intelligence...

I was working as a junior reporter on the local paper by then. It wasn't the most exciting job covering flower shows and missing dogs, but the editor – who played golf with my father – also allowed me to write a weekly horoscope column. Krystal and I had lost all contact with Rupert Haut-Dougbreah by then, but I knew he'd finished university and was now in chambers in London. I made an excuse to go to London for the day and phoned to get an appointment with him. Of course, I needed a reason to do that, so I gave a false name and said I was seeking a divorce. I wasn't sure whether it was for unreasonable drunkenness or insanity of my imaginary spouse, so said it was for both. The telephonist was a little unsure whether a junior barrister would be qualified to handle this, so I name-dropped my connections to the Royal Family, laid on the aristocratic style of speech, and of course she gave me an appointment. Sometimes being a Jollybottom gives one an edge in these matters.

Rupert wasn't terribly impressed when I made my entrance into his office. In fact, his little round face was rather red and cross when he saw me, but I didn't let that scare me and instead concentrated on the job in hand. It was a difficult conversation, but I was as delicate as possible and avoided using any unpleasant terms. I did however threaten to make his predilections public unless he showed some kindness towards my sister and kept our names out of the newspapers.

The conversation didn't take long. I went over it again and again on the train journey home. I understood how some people might view what

I'd done as unethical, might possibly even call it blackmail? They were the types however who wouldn't understand the deep code of honour all the Jollybottoms had to adhere to. Not so much *noblesse oblige* as *salvis faciem omnibus modis*. Rupert was eventually able to see my viewpoint, obviously.

The eventual court case of Keeler v Regina took place in 1963. Many of the lesser mortals who had been at Cliveden that weekend were in attendance, while the dignitaries and VIPs were discreetly absent. I was living in London by then and went along to the Old Bailey to see it played out. I'd tried to get back in touch with Mandy a couple of times, but her contact details were probably out of date by now and I'd received no follow up from the phone messages I'd left. When I did see her again, she was in the dock.

On the next day the papers salaciously ran with nearly all the names of the players, especially the minor ones such as the "other girls". One was referred to as Miss X, "who due to her being under the age of majority was prevented from being named". Rupert had kept his word, pulled his strings, kept our names out of it, and the whole Jollybottom clan would always be grateful to him. In today's world of course it doesn't matter a jot how one lives one's life, but in those days, it was important to protect one's reputation and avoid the irreparable damage that could be caused. He did what had to be done, our family name was untarnished, and most importantly, the truth of Rupert's predilections was never exposed. Having a homosexual in the family – well frankly, every decent family had to have one. Many a Jollybottom *"confirmed bachelor"* had trod the boards and entertained the British Empire throughout the generations. It was a mark of good breeding and good family connections. But to be a vegetarian! Just imagine the outcome then if people had learned this about him. Raised in a family of Norman conquering butchers – unthinkable. It was still only the 1960s after all.

Libra Sun Sign cuttings

And speaking of neurotics, here in Libra we find the ultimate Sturm und Drang (look it up) of the human psyche. How can they deliver bad news, impose their control, and generally make someone angry without losing that person's love and adoration? I must admit the vacillations of this astrological tribe has driven many a Jollybottom to the edge of reason. Librans have innate charm and vivacity but are also blindingly dishonest and deceitful. All done in a lovely way, of course. And, despite the rumour, they know only too well the importance of hard work, just if they can get someone else to do it for them. So, if you handle their P.R., or you're a stylist for a Libran, they'll love every little thing you do for them and their image. In fact, many of them find second careers in these areas, when their own performing days are over. Being note perfect year after year is exhausting, but a Libran thrives on finding new ways to make someone look fabulous, darling!

Sometimes it is hard to be an astrologer. One's raison d'être is to divine the mysteries and messages of the planets, however unpleasant or unwelcome these may turn out to be. Every sun-sign has its negative and positive, and light and shade. So, when it comes to a fair assessment of Libra, and the sign itself is, of course, the cipher for justice, it behoves me to mention the many good qualities these characters potentially possess. The great Mrs Thatcher for example springs to mind as an example of fearless independence and single-mindedness. That great lady showed the way in how the sign of Libra may use their skills in successful world domination. Often however the inclination in Librans to swing means they will do anything and anyone to maintain the status quo and keep their interests secure. And sorry to say, much of the peacekeeping is done on their backs.

Jolly Astrolly! Website, 2012

LET'S LOOK AT LIBRA!

Libra is an air sign. In terms of sporting activity this means they enjoy hot air ballooning, hang gliding and wind-surfing – so long as the wind doesn't spoil their hair. They are a sign which works well in a partnership, so any form of graceful movement – preferably in a nice outfit – such as dancing, gymnastics or paired synchronised swimming is perfect. An important consideration however is that Libra's partner must be inferior in some way. Almost certainly the partnership thrives if the non-Libran is physically inept, repellent to look at, and/or socially awkward. Put simply, anyone bad can only make Libra look better, and that, in a nutshell, is the Libran mission statement.

Round the U Bend with Maud, Plumber's Weekly, 1979

♓

CHAPTER 3

Pisces

St Tropez, 1968

I can remember the sweet smell of the bougainvillea in Antibes as if it was yesterday. The sunshine and that rich blue ocean, so famously captured in the paintings of Matisse and Cezanne are fixed in my memories. It was 1968 and the South of France was the most magical, hippest place to spend the summer. By this time, I was in with the In Crowd baby! I had been invited to stay in a chateau not too far from the coast. The invite was extended by my lovely musician friends – I was to be part of their "groovy" entourage. I can hear you ask – why exactly *were you there*, Maud? Well, I'd become known in fashion circles for my flair in organising fashion shoots – I was what would later become known as a "stylist". My most successful photo shoot had been for a new teenage girl magazine, *Dollypop*, when my contacts in the pop world had helped me secure a massive scoop – the front cover and a two-page spread featuring the face of '68, Paul Sinclair, and a bevy of famous teenage models. This had been great for my bank account and my reputation. I'd even tried my hand at a little bit of modelling myself, and although it had been fun wearing those delicious clothes, I found it boring standing around for ages, being primped and powdered under hot lights, and being man-handled into unnatural positions. No, I felt my talents were better spent helping people to achieve their potential, and by offering them the very best advice. I felt, it was almost a duty, even a calling, to tell people what to do, and the best time to do it. I was considered "simpatico" by my fashion world co-workers, from the photographer down to the lowliest runner, and often found myself calling on my astrological gifts to help develop these often lost, and somewhat fragile creatures, advising and nurturing them as my skills compelled me.

I'd heard that Paul Sinclair was going to be in the south of France at the same time as my little crowd. He'd come across as a sweet boy to work with, and had a fabulous reputation for his guitar skills, but he did appear as slightly neurotic and needing careful handling to bring out his best side. The *Dollypop* shoot had been successful, but slightly exhausting to arrange. But here *en vacances* I put the exertions behind me, and concentrated on perfecting my French, my tan, and any useful connections. As well as being the staff astrologer at *Dollypop*, I was allowed to contribute the occasional show biz story, so it was a working holiday of a sort.

We would spend the days on the beach, and dance away the nights in *Saint-Tropez* and *Juan les Pins*. We were always bumping into Mick and Keith and the boys – or should I be naughty and say they were always bumping into us? We were, after all, the main attraction. I was pleased when I eventually managed to "bump" into Paul Sinclair for the second time. We were all spending the day on the beach in St Tropez. He had a small entourage with him, including his girlfriend and another couple, and we waved at one another and later met for a paddle. I was pleased when Paul agreed to stroll with me for a little astrological *tete-a-tete*. Pleased but also a little alarmed that he insisted on wearing water wings, in case of being swept out to sea. The sun was warm but not too fierce. It was still before noon and the sand was cool and damp under our feet. I was just happy to be in that moment, when I noticed Paul suddenly making slight, jerky movements as he stepped carefully along the water edge. It transpired that Paul had a phobia about seaweed and crustaceans and was performing some sort of hopping/swerving manoeuvre to avoid contact with them. I wondered at his choice of a beach holiday but then remembered the presence of his manager.

This may sound like uncharacteristic boasting on my part, but I believe my astrological counselling on that day reached into the unstable emotional inner mess of Paul Sinclair and pulled out a winner! By explaining his sun sign of Pisces and emphasising his connection to all things oceanic, Paul was strengthened and ready to accept his many challenges. Not only was I able to convince him to tackle his phobias and embrace his love of sea-life, he manfully ripped off his water wings and strode back to his friends a Sea God – Neptune himself! So successful was this impromptu counselling on my part it encouraged me to consider this the first chapter in the book I was going to write, *"Myth, Magic and Maud – How to Reach for the Stars!"*.

A week later it was a personal triumph when myself and my friends were given VIP passes to the nightclub *Le Marine* in *Antibes*. Two thirds of Spinal Tap, one Trogg, half a Beatle and Paul Sinclair were playing a hastily arranged concert to raise awareness for the plight of sea molluscs. Like millions of others, until then I was selfishly unaware of the sea mollusc plight, but now it seemed the situation was redeemable by the best and brightest of 1968's rock champions. And I hope I don't appear boastful by mentioning my major part in this.

Before the concert, which was to be the highlight of the evening, the nightclub was filling up with the great and the glamorous. Sasha and Dionne were here with their crowd, and the dance floor was crowded. I remember meeting a young blonde French woman in the Ladies' room, obviously upset and in need of a friendly word. She was a nice, shy girl who sadly hadn't been blessed with much in the way of looks. I implored her not to let this curb her style and told her in no uncertain terms how to make the best of herself.

This plain young woman with little self confidence in herself was now doubting her boyfriend's sincerity. He had been spotted on the dance floor enwrapped around a woman apparently called Yoko. When Brigitte, as I discovered she was called, saw him in this intimate embrace she fled for the powder room, despite his insistence he was just attempting the latest dance move, "*le Poulpe*".[1] Once I discovered Brigitte's boyfriend's sun sign was Scorpio, I was able to give her a good pep talk, tell her where she was going wrong and the best way to handle him. I told her to put on a brave smile, ooze with va va voom, and make it clear to Yoko that her time in the spotlight was over – she wasn't going to break up anyone's relationship. Time for Brigitte[2] to shake her Gallic bottom and win back her boyfriend's attentions.

The concert was amazing. *Le Marine* was packed, even the local dignitaries attended, and the surprise supergroup[3] put together in days, starring Paul Sinclair and some others was a huge success. Even today, bootleg tapes are in circulation. Sadly, this was to be Paul's last appearance musically. After our session together on the beach he gave up this career and retired to Bali where he perfected a design called a Flotation Tank. He also wrote a brief memoir about his days as a born-again fish. I think it's fair to say the embracing of his inner Pisces was almost entirely due to my influence.

---

[1] For fans of cinematic trivia, the dance was immortalised in the 1990s film "*Poulpe Fiction*"

[2] I was delighted when I learned later that summer Brigitte, was to marry her German boyfriend, "Gunter", who had given up dancing in nightclubs and had instead, after his inspirational meeting with me, taken up astrology. **Sachs, Gunter:** *The Astrology File: Scientific Proof of the Link Between Star Signs and Human Behaviour.* Orion Books (December 1999).

[3] That acclaimed line-up in full: David St. Hubbins, Derek Smalls, Reg Presley, Ronnie Bond, Stu Sutcliffe and the Sea God himself, Paul Sinclair

Pisces Sun Sign cuttings

Pisces is another sign that finds an educational experience enriching as a holiday choice, especially if this coincides with their twin compulsions of complete exhibitionism (or acting, as they prefer to call it), and drinking themselves unconscious. Any sort of watery drama festival will do but just find one staged in a rain forest, sponsored by Stella Artois, and you can expect Olympic standard sobbing and histrionics off the Richter scale. Just the ticket for Pisces! Keen cineastes will spot the potential cinematic plot in this situation so expect to see the final creative piece advertised as *"grand guignol"* and masterfully directed by Werner Herzog. It promises to run at the BFI for the next thirty years.

As Pisces dwells in the element of fluidity we can say with certainty they are destined to be alcoholics. If this is not enough to deal with, they also have a very shaky grasp of reality and are dreamy and artistic by nature. If you live in London, you've probably come upon them somewhere damp and unpleasant. Many of those who once held thespian ambitions can be found stumbling around in the vicinity of the Royal Court Theatre, London where they once appeared in something "ground-breaking" and "radical". The outlook for Pisces is a little tricky this year as grumpy old Saturn takes root until 2017. As the solar eclipse also occurs this year in Pisces, the last sign of the zodiac, this is a very important era for casting off the unnecessary and completing outstanding transactions. It will be a time of uncovering, and revelation. Try not to do this on a crowded tube train. Another revelation will be how much punishment the liver of a Pisces can take, so get professional help in other words.

Jolly Astrolly! **Website, April 2016**

Pisces

The Sign of the Fish
February 20th – March 20th

When they're not gazing at their reflections or planning their next scuba diving holiday on your credit card, they're draping themselves in silver and sobbing because they can't find Nemo. Don't be fooled by this soft-soap nonsense. In reality they are ruthless, scaly creatures with slippery modus operandi (always unpleasant) and a switchblade in their underpants.

Many human beings experience emotional changes with the wax and wane of the moon. Pisceans are almost always slightly unhinged at the best of times – during a full moon they are best avoided unless you carry a stun gun and defibrillator. Far too costly when travelling Ryanair.

Blue Yonder Travel Magazine, 2014

♍

CHAPTER 4

Virgo

Walthamstow, 1974

The early 1970s were quite a grim time. The UK seemed to be in conflict with itself, as disputes between the government and trade unions caused the economy to implode, and society began to look dangerously out of control. In 1972 the miner's strike led to the eventual "three-day week" whereby electricity was rationed, and power cuts were common. It was a miserable, grey time for most of the population – but not for Maud! By this time, I was working on a freelance basis, quite successfully, with some of the top names in fashion as a stylist. I specialised in working for the glossy magazines, but with the occasional foray into newspapers and other outlets. I had a good rep with the top photographers, and they knew I could pull a shoot together, leaving them free to indulge their artistic talents.

It was in a meeting at the offices of *Swan* – a glossy mag that was part of the Collins Nash empire. The production team and myself were at a brainstorming session searching for location settings. The photographer of the day, Orlando Swelt, had sent his assistant Edward along with a clear message on the sort of thing he wanted for the Autumn/Winter shoot.

Edward, a charming former public-school boy, spoke quietly but intensely on Orlando's behalf. It seemed the maestro wanted to capture the zeitgeist of disharmony and anarchy, class differences were tearing the country apart and it was the responsibility of the fashion industry to acknowledge and show this. Where would the location be that would best reflect this? What Orlando really wanted, Edward told us, was a display of opposite values – luxury clothes in a setting of poverty. The obscenity of luxury couture as the French used to call it, before they lost their pre-eminence in the fashion world. It was important to reinforce solidarity with the miners, the electricity workers, the trade unions, the downtrodden public servants. Everyone in the meeting nodded their heads. Everyone except the team accountant who had signed off Orlando's contract at £500.00 per day.

There was a lot of discussion about suitable locations. The power cuts presented problems in time wasting long journeys out of London, although there were several requests for "up north, somewhere". The shoot had to be done and dusted within one day – paying accommodation costs for models and their handlers would rack up the budget. The accountant looked uncomfortable.

Edward reiterated Orlando's request for grittiness, deprivation, and some squalor if it could be arranged (Orlando was always keen on squalor). Emily, a young production assistant suggested the East End – she'd never been there, and had in fact grown up in Weybridge, but felt it had the right sort of vibe? In the end the location was decided on – it had to be Walthamstow market.

Which is how I found myself sitting in a pie and eel cafe in Walthamstow market, on a cold, dark morning in February. The cafe owner was in turns perplexed, irritated, and confused by the sudden invasion of fashion people in his premises. He switched on a megawatt smile for the models however, and with a few promises of his photo getting in the magazine he accommodated the crowd. I'd arranged the use of his cafe as a base over the phone and I don't think he realised what the whole operation would mean. The models used a trailer as a changing room – parking this and a partner trailer for make-up and hairdressing while the market was trading made the stallholders a little tetchy, but I bought up some fabulous sari fabric from a couple of them and made good with the petty cash in soothing gestures which helped things along. *Swan* had always been generous in covering my expenses.

The shoot had started early – not as early as the market stalls, but before there were loads of shoppers around. The day was dreary and despite the big location lights on full beam, the lights from the stalls helped supplement the sets. Orlando had insisted on shooting while the market was in full flow. The local police had agreed to the disruption way in advance, but had queried why this couldn't take place on a quieter day? I had to phrase my response carefully. There was no way I wanted to answer, "*because the photographer wanted to see the creative energy a chaotic symbiosis of wealth and poverty can release*". I went with "*we want it a bit lively*", instead. I knew how to use my "nice face" from a very early age.

The models were complaining about the cold when out of earshot of Orlando. He held a lot of status in their world – upset him and the chances of working with him again were slight. On this occasion he was using very tall girls from a mixture of backgrounds – all colours and races in order to show off the beautiful ethnic inspired designs that would showcase the following autumn's trends. Shoppers queuing up for their fruit and veg were taken aback when an elegant, long limbed beauty wearing Dior and woolly fingerless gloves weighed out (under supervision), five pounds of Maris Pipers and a large cauliflower. The fabric stall was even more of a surprise. One model was stretched out across the rolls of material in a weird, crucifixion pose, her voluminous sleeves draped artistically. It looked uncomfortable and back breaking, but her Ossie Clark flowing outfit complimented the stall's offerings strikingly. Orlando may have been a pretentious, nonsense spouting nitwit, but he did have a dramatically creative eye.

I was kept busy running between stalls, cafe, and the trailers. I thought the day was going fairly well despite the grey clouds and crowd management when disaster struck. The lights in all the shops, cafes and market stalls went off. The sound of Slade blaring from the record stall suddenly stopped – the power had been cut.

Creative heads huddled together while Mr Stan, the cafe owner, glowered from the doorway. Stall holders seemed philosophic in the face of uncertainty. And then a slight drizzle started to patter the tarpaulin roofs of the market stalls. Edward spoke to me quietly away from Orlando and the team. *"We may be able to use what we already have, but a few interiors would help"*. I thought about this and asked if the location lights would work inside the cafe. Edward shook his head. I told him to go into the cafe with the others while I racked my brain for a solution.

I'd done a site visit two weeks before and walked the entire market and back to really get to grips with it. It was huge, rumoured to be visible from space along with the Great Wall of China. I remembered one particular stall down at the far end, selling all sorts of religious tokens and knick knacks. Everything on the stall was arranged in clear categories – by sizes and by item and looked extremely clean and dusted – the whole market stall shone with devotion, in all ways. And there were plenty of candles. Votive candles, pillar candles, candles in special holders illustrating saints and the Virgin Mary – all were to be found on Frankie's stall. I made a quick decision and arranged to buy the whole lot. We would light up Mr. Stan's Cafe in a blaze of holy light and make those models look heavenly!

I rushed back to Mr Stan's and quickly spoke with Edward. A few different expressions passed over his features but finally he smiled, nervously and told me to leave it with him. And less than two hours later, Mr Stan's pie and mash emporium was bathed in golden light from a hundred flickering candles. After a few mishaps with the models' make-up as it was awkwardly applied by torch light, and their rippling but flammable pre-Raphaelite locks, Orlando was able to weave his magic and make his angels look authentic. The theme had changed; it was no longer the disharmony of luxury and poverty; it was now the sacred and the profane. Or at least this is what Orlando said in a later interview in The Guardian (Manchester, not Walthamstow).

I was so grateful to Frankie with his religious curiosities and funny south American accent, and he was grateful to me – together we had saved the day and he had managed to make a bit extra for his long-term ambitions. It seemed his dream was to join the priesthood – who knew one needed a nest egg put by to do that? I did find out however he was born under Virgo, which made a lot of things clearer.

And one day, a long, long way ahead of us in 2013, no one was prouder when, along with the rest of the world, I saw those dreams realised as the white smoke ascended over the Vatican. The next Holy Father was Pope Francis. I like to think I played a small, but crucial part in that extraordinary journey.

Virgo Sun Sign cuttings

MUSICAL VIRGO

I sometimes drift back to my teenage spell in a Surrey convent. The place was, I think it fair to say, an early exponent in aversion therapy. Many times, a mental image of Sister Hepatitis comes to mind, most often in a violent flashback when I pass a nearby drain and smell disinfectant. Sometimes she floats back to me in dreams where I awake in a cold sweat with violent trembling. When all is said and done however, I do hold a sneaking admiration for the woman and have tried to replicate her methods in much of my own career. After all, even old Maud is prone to the occasional prod of sentimentality.

Sister Hepatitis had been incarcerated in St Cuthbert's for several years before I fell into her clutches. Single-mindedly driven in her pursuit of hygienic perfection, and more than proficient in the lesser-known martial arts, Sister Hep was a role model for her vocation. That woman, and I admit to welling up as I write this, was legendary in her execution of a *Vileda* mop and bucket cut and thrust. It was a move never likely to be seen in an Olympic stadium but unforgettable to those who witnessed it. No germ ever dared to multiply where that Angel of Mercy spread her *Domestos*. If one woman can typify a high-intensity Virgo, Sister Hepatitis is that female. Although sometimes Virgos are male. I'll leave you with your thoughts on this.

Dear God, where do we start with neurotic Virgo? Critical, analytical and fault finding; all can be positive traits in a musician seeking the perfect performance. Let them wind themselves up into a frenzy of indecisive angst however, and nothing will go according to the Virgoan master plan, of which they hatch many in their lives. Try to stop them interacting with other Virgos, and never let them breed. The phrase "anal retentive" was invented for the resulting offspring of that hellish alliance. Having said that, so long as you keep the rehearsal room biochemically cleaned and run the practice schedules to a timetable Mussolini would have been proud of, you have every chance of hearing some great music produced by a Virgo. Earthy, sensual, and sublime; see Van Morrison, B.B. King, Branford Marsalis. Just forget about all that Virgin nonsense.

Being the most neurotic of the twelve signs, Virgo enjoys any pursuit leading to self-realisation, calmness, and inner and outer perfection. Since these are difficult goals to reach Virgo will thrive on any self-sacrifice necessary to achieve them. Tai chi, yoga and anything requiring intricate, repetitive actions are best for Virgo. They are happiest when denying themselves normal functions such as eating and drinking and contact with other humans. If their physical quest for perfection demands seven years in Tibet, then Virgo is first at the check-in desk with a weightless sports bag and a signed copy of Mahatma Gandhi's Fitness Video. Failing that a hunger strike in solitary confinement would be just the job.

Riffin' with Maud, From The Riff Magazine, October 2018

⚊⚊

CHAPTER 5

Gemini

Eurovision Song Contest, 1983

In 1983 it was my great honour to represent the United Kingdom at the Eurovision Song Contest, in Berlin. Not in any official capacity exactly but as a bona fide member of the support team to the Space Hunterz, the group of three boys and three girls picked to win for Great Britain in this giant, superannuated end-of-the-pier show.

I was playing my integral part as the team's astrologer and doing my best work as a pop star wrangler; skills I'd honed over many years of hanging around, calming down creatives, massaging the egos and making myself indispensable. The Space Hunterz were being groomed for stardom in the music business. They were all in their twenties, clean looking with shiny teeth and, fortunately, a couple of them could sing. More importantly, they looked right, were confident and came alive in front of a TV camera. Off camera they weren't such a harmonious ensemble. Gregory, a dark-haired young man, didn't seem at ease with the other five, and kept himself aloof as much as he could. His offhand manner was explained away as "nerves" and "stage fright" – certainly the stage set of a medieval castle wall and having to climb it while dressed like an astronaut and singing drivel didn't help him with this. Their music director clearly had undisclosed mental health issues as he had envisaged them as interplanetary explorers accidentally popping up in the Middle Ages. Nothing in the dire song they were there to sing gave any clue as to why this had happened. That none of this made sense posed no problem for Eurovision viewers, but the fact that the space girls wore high heels and odd sparkly leotards seemed ridiculously sexist even for those days. They didn't sing much either, just making an odd beeping noise now and again as they wiggled their sparkly bottoms. Not much space exploring for them, it seemed.

I have to come clean and say my boyfriend of the time, Adam, was a BBC employee, and was there at the Eurovision for legitimate work purposes. At least, I think he was. Of a sort. Not necessarily there for BBC work, as such, but we'll come to that later. At the time I was happy to be cited on his generous expense account as a "special consultant" – in 1983 the BBC were very accommodating around this sort of thing. I also occasionally worked for the Beeb as a freelance photo researcher, but interestingly I had met Adam through my sister. Krystal had made all sorts of connections from her dancing days, and somehow, she had stayed in touch with Adam – or he had bothered to stay in touch with her – for many years.

Nowadays her skills were fully utilised choreographing a troupe of dancing poodles. It was very seasonal work as usually she was restricted to seaside shows, with the occasional pantomime at Christmas, but Krystal's Canine Cuties always stole the show. She'd kept her 60s blonde beehive hairdo upright through two marriages and fourteen poodles, but now changed its colour each season with the dogs' fur to match and would probably have carried on doing so until the RSPCA intervened. Somehow Adam had pulled some magical BBC strings and Krystal was also here with us at the Euro bun fight, minus the Cuties.

Looking back, Krystal also being allowed at Eurovision was more than a little strange. She wasn't a BBC employee, and had no official reason to be there, but Adam had arranged everything so that she was included. He only smiled mysteriously when I asked him if this was all above board? Wouldn't the licence fee payers be angry about his elastic expenses account?

Somehow, two Jollybottoms at Eurovision seemed not to pose a problem to Adam, so Krystal joined us, and the poodles kicked back in doggy day care for a week, growing their roots out at the same time.

But back to Adam. He was a charming, funny man in his late twenties, who led a somewhat mysterious life. He was confident in a calm, decisive way, and I could imagine him as the soldier he had once been, after a degree at Cambridge. With no apparent spousal or offspring baggage, he led a solitary life both at work and at home. His job was a senior Facilities and Processes Manager, or sometimes a Processes and Facilities Manager, and he was very well thought of for his superb Facilitating and Processing Skills, if only people knew what these exactly were. He didn't seem to have a regular office – he was hotdesking decades before the term existed – and strangely his phone number was never listed in the BBC global office directory. He always said he was based in the World Service building in the Strand, where the staff canteen produced glorious international cuisine, but I had never met him there for lunch, and was never introduced to any of his colleagues. I enjoyed the times we spent together, but never expected anything further or more committed than how we were then. I wasn't interested in a long-term partnership – I was too self-driven to contemplate a life shared with anyone else, and I felt too old now, at 42, to give it a shot. God knows my sister and brother took up enough of my emotional energy. There was also no getting away from the fact that Adam was much, much younger than me.

Looking back, everything I knew about Adam was hazy, but I did know his date of birth, and therefore his sun sign. He appeared well educated and smart and was very knowledgeable about politics on the international scale, but I steered clear of discussing this to avoid displaying my ignorance. He never spoke about his family, except to say he'd followed in his father's footsteps in joining the army – I never met any of his relatives. He had friends from university who occasionally turned up on BBC comedy shows, and these were of great interest to me and my future ambitions. Adam was funny and charming in a self-deprecating way, but always, inevitably evasive. This added to his charm, and frankly I was too busy with my own concerns to delve into his deepest, darkest secrets. The main thing was he always appeared happy to support me, emotionally and financially, in my unorthodox career. That counted for a huge amount. I was desperate, desperate to have an astrology slot on TV. I used every trick in the astrologer's almanac to impress him and his friends with my talents, stage presence and unshakeable self-confidence. In truth my carefully choreographed pushiness was probably obnoxious, but I hung on determinedly to see this campaign through to the bitter end. There would be a Jollybottom on daytime TV in the 1980s, it was my destiny, whatever the planets said. No point in wasting time by being too timid about it.

On the day of the final rehearsal, we sat around for ages in the green room, trying to calm the nerves of the Space Hunterz. Gregor, in particular, was very fidgety and found every excuse he could to leave the room. I asked Adam to keep an eye on him, but he was also acting a little odd and disappearing every now and again. He said he was speaking with the technicians, and I didn't question it given his job title.

I was quite flattered when a member of a German TV crew seemed to recognise me from somewhere. It turned out that Juergen had remembered me from a photoshoot in Hamburg back in the 70s. He was with a team shooting a little film at Eurovision, a light and fluffy thing showing the build up to the big event. He wanted me to do a short piece to camera. He remembered how I'd given zodiac readings the last time we'd met. I was a bit hesitant – only, of course a teeny bit – but my German wasn't very good, and I worried I might fluff it up. Juergen reassured me they would subtitle my speech – they only wanted a few short, pithy "Maud" type astrological predictions – a brief, funny piece to fill in bits between coverage of the acts. Juergen was persuasive so I agreed and spent a hurried hour putting a few thoughts together.

The technical rehearsal was going on noisily in the background, and film cameras veered back and forward across the massive stage area. In our section, the UK would be sharing with Spain and Ireland, so the medieval castle wall had to appear out of a bullring and then morph into a cocktail bar. It was distracting but Juergen assured me the background noise would be edited out, so I went ahead with my lively, yet thoughtful piece to Juergen's video camera, delivered with a winning smile. I was in my element, of course. Between takes, I had half an eye on the Valencian bull-ring in front of me being dismantled furiously, and the medieval Windsor Castle replacing it. The singers were herded at the side of the stage in their costumes, and the Space Hunterz contingent were down to five. The two boys trooped onto the stage with the three girls tottering behind them. They looked stupid but I gave them full marks for trying. But where was the missing boy?

Juergen cued me in once again and I started my spiel. I gave a few general predictions, nothing legally threatening, and to my surprise a few German phrases surfaced from the past. To my greater surprise however, as the wall was now up and five Space Hunterz were in their spots, a young man wearing an astronaut suit ran on stage and up the ramparts to the top. In his haste, the whole set wobbled dangerously, someone screamed – a Euro scream – and an earth tremor gripped medieval England. A Space Hunting girl was wobbled off and out of her shoes. This mad scene was bad enough when one of the boys – I assumed it was Gregor – suddenly made a flying leap from the ramparts as if on strings, landed in a perfect fall and rolled gymnastically across the stage floor and into the wings. My mouth dropped open mid speech. I couldn't take my eyes away from the stage although I could still hear Juergen speaking to me.

I heard him repeat the question, with typical German politeness, "so Maud, do you have a prediction tonight?"

I couldn't reply to this, or even begin to summon up some waffle, as to my astonishment, a man looking very much like my boyfriend Adam now ran from somewhere left of the stage, across it and into the wings after Gregor.

I was transfixed. The only thing I could remember saying in disbelief as the set crumbled and chaos unfolded in front of me, was "… the wall is coming down!" A prophecy, made in Berlin, which turned out to be one of my best, as it happened. I was right about us not winning Eurovision, as well.

Gemini Sun Sign cuttings

Gemini

This is the year when Gemini must either move home or sort out a difficult domestic situation. Combine this with their strong interest in democratic processes and how to subvert them, and you understand why their neighbours complain regularly about the number of third world dictators they are harbouring in their garden sheds. No other sign, apart from Leo, has the skill for self-promotion like a Gemini, and many can be found running for local government posts and talking themselves into positions of high office. You can always hear a Gemini approaching in the corridors of power by the clanking of their mayoral chains, and their PR entourage creeping just behind them.

Your Local Council magazine, March 1998

Badass Gemini

Hip hop, trip hop, flip flop, and chip shop – if there's a message to be broadcast to the masses, vocal Gemini is the one to do it. By the way I made the last two up, as Maud rarely ventures into the "grimy" end of anything, thank you very much. Geminis – the Twins – are a quick-witted bunch, spontaneous and entertaining, and can tune up the ambience in the dullest of venues. They do have their serious side, however, and you'd be mistaken if you took their happy face onstage for granted. An often-frustrating aspect to this sign is their seeming cooperation with others, frequently undermined by discovery of some backdoor Gemini self-promotion. Don't be surprised to find out Gemini has a secret solo publicity event scheduled – and who else in the zodiac would have the brass neck to ask your opinion afterwards re those glossy head shots? It's not so much *diva* syndrome, as *running* with the fox, but *hunting* with the hounds. Something we do quite a lot in Clenching, to the confusion of our visitors.

The double-edged sword of Gemini – how much of a dollop of topsy-turvy can you stand in a chap? Either he's chattering like a chimp in Chinatown, or he's broody like a Brutus in bromide. Whichever side of the coin lands face up, he or she will talk their way out of anything including third degree murder and lesser transgressions, and never knowingly relate an honest story if they can help it. The fact that they articulate most of their adventures to themselves, loudly, in the street, accompanied by howls of maniacal laughter can be disconcerting but it means they never need to actively seek out company. Unless, of course, the "black dog" of gloomy Gemini makes his or her presence felt, in which case hide any sharp knives and ask the pharmacist for arnica suppositories. In summary, they can be entertaining but are often exhausting and usually pathological liars.

Gemini prefers team activity to solitary pursuits – if there's no-one on the receiving end of their superior knowledge it's a wasted enterprise. They love to talk, and are happiest lecturing, coaching, and giving instructions. Schooldays may bring unhappy memories for Gemini as cut-throat competition with the PE teacher often resulted in a long-distance cross-country run in the snow. These days fitness classes and gym sessions brings out the verbal dexterity of Gemini, even if unqualified. A true Gemini is never put off instructing so long as they perceive a receptive audience. Perceive is the keyword here.

Yo Grime Website – M. Jollybottom, Guest Editor, April-May edition, 2015

♑

CHAPTER 6

Capricorn

Berlin, late 1980s

The Final Crossing

Last week saw the sad demise of the ground-breaking publication, *"Crossings"* – or *"Kreuzungen"* as it was originally called at its launch in Berlin, 1985. Founded by the multi-media genius Juergen Muller and his English girlfriend of the time, Maud Jollybottom, the monthly magazine grew to become the voice box of the age – capturing the zeitgeist and disseminating it across Europe. To say the magazine was influential is to underplay its importance in 1980s cold war east and west Europe. New trends in music and fashion, both on the catwalk and out on the street, all had their debut recorded in the magazine everyone had to follow if they were anyone. The creatives loved it, and advertising in it became essential to the numerous companies that supported it and kept it afloat financially. And it did have a rocky start – Muller was widely reported as saying he gambled with both his flat – the magazine's birthplace – and his ex-wife's home in West Berlin, without her knowledge of his chicanery in getting his project launched.

Daytime television astrologer Jollybottom seems an unlikely pairing with the creative dynamo Muller, but during the 80s she was often spotted on the coat tails of the fashion scene and had sound euro credentials. She'd met Muller years before at a pop launch for a teenage magazine, and the two eventually *angekoppelt*[1] after mysterious Maud moved into the flat with him over the "dry cleaners" in the *Schoneberg* neighbourhood. Still resonant with Bowie[2] connections, the area was alive with left field music venues and punk bars – thoroughly decadent, druggy, and drunk to excess and yet miraculously giving birth to some of the most exciting artistic output of the decade. Despite the hard start, Muller, and later Jollybottom, produced the European creative voice of the 1980s, and the crossings from fringe to mainstream are now legendary in publishing history.

Except from Time Out Magazine, June 1998

Excerpt from Obituary: Juergen Miller

… Some of the more outlandish claims about Jollybottom and Miller during this period include the rumours of international espionage. This relates to the time in the mid to late 1980s when she reputedly worked in a "dry cleaner" in *Hochbeiner Strasse*, West Berlin. This was during the politically febrile 1980s, and the major players in cold war tactics aligned themselves on the world stage. Paranoia in Moscow about the West's intentions meant espionage and information gathering was at a new height, and Jollybottom's accounts of her mysterious Germanic spell remain hidden in a haze of dry-cleaning steam. We only know for certain the pair were based in Berlin during the 1980s and, like Jollybottom' s alleged former mentee David Bowie, she would go on to describe this period as her most creative and explorative …

The Guardian, 2014

---

[1]   Coupled, English translation.

[2]   *Spiders from Mars*, by David Bowie. Inspired by M. Jollybottom

Transcript of Interview with Maud Jollybottom, for *My Country Home magazine*

"First of all, Maud, let me say how lovely your Cotswold home is, and how tastefully you have decorated it". Is that a genuine Arts and Crafts chair?"

"It is – well spotted! I picked it up in an auction in Nether Crushing. Thank you, Gabi, it's been a real labour of love, I can tell you. We are so lucky living here, in this glorious part of the world – I can't imagine living anywhere else!"

"And yet, older readers may connect you with the magazine Crossings, which I believe saw you based in Berlin in the 1980s?"

"I was based in Berlin for a few years while the magazine was getting off the ground. I like to look back on it as a really creative time – much like darling David (Bowie) did a few years before me. Actually, I feel in many ways so similar to David, both equally creative, both fascinated by the universe and distinct from ordinary souls. My Berlin years were just as productive as his, maybe more so.

"And yet, in some ways, you have seemed reluctant when asked to expand on what you actually did there, during the Berlin days?

"Well, to begin with, it was a tiny operation with the founder, Juergen, running the magazine from his apartment. I helped him out with my contacts, wrote some of the editorial, and generally mucked in. I was also writing astrology columns that were syndicated so we were both kept busy. I miss doing the predictive stuff in a way – now I only do it during personal consultations. The minutia of everyday lives has no interest for me. Berlin was an exciting place to be then, but now I relish my quiet time here amongst friends and family – I include the cat when I say family! **(Maud's cat Debo is purring in her lap while she speaks).** We both helped out very occasionally in the dry cleaners, of course, when they were short staffed … we were friendly with the owners and lived right above the place – it would have been rude not to … only sticking a few tickets here and there, not *tenderising*[3] the lederhosen you understand.

And that dry cleaning shop seems to be the basis of the spying rumours that have surfaced recently – can I ask you Maud, what is your response to these rumours – they do sound a bit "*Tinker Tailor*!"

Laughter "… how funny! I can't believe this old fairy story has been rehashed. It was so sad to hear about Juergen's passing – his own <u>crossing</u> if you like, (**Maud dabs her eyes with Debo's tail**) – but it seems to have generated interest again in all those silly stories …"

"Of course, Juergen – did you have any inkling when you first met him how successful he was likely to be?

"Not at first, no – we met at a photo shoot for a pop band in London and he seemed to be in charge of everything … just another bossy German, I thought. Actually, he was really skilled in so many things like camera work, styling, PR – he had excellent English and was a mass of energy, but I didn't appreciate all his capabilities, then. He could always think of the right thing to say, the right catchphrase – instantly quotable! He was known as *Juergen the Sleurgan* in the London advertising world, everyone wanted to employ him. He was a complicated man underneath though, and always climbing a mountain in the way all Capricorns do.

"Why do you say that? My mother's a Capricorn!"

They can be tough to live with. And a Capricorn with Virgo rising is really hard work. Even with someone as easy going as me! (**More laughter**) Juergen relished being the editor of Crossings, and really, he preferred to go it alone. It took me years to appreciate he wasn't cut out to be in a

---

[3]   "*Tenderising*" is a German dry-cleaning term, often used in treating leather garments, such as *lederhosen*. It was also used as a euphemism in German spy circles when the exchange of an East German citizen with the West did not go as planned – to avoid undue speculation the unlucky East German national was usually "*tenderised*" by the Stasi.

couple. When we first got together his marriage to Helga had just ended and he was obsessed with proving his worth to her. I suppose I felt sorry for him – she refused to let their son visit him at weekends because Juergen would insist on spraying him with antiseptic every time he saw him. I was drawn though towards him and his world – it was exciting and opened new avenues for me. Juergen was fuelled by all this nervous energy. That comes from having Virgo as a rising sign. Living above a dry cleaner didn't help with his anxieties. He often complained about his face turning blue from the chemical fumes coming up through the floorboards. He did have a slight blue tinge about him sometimes, but I put this down to a heart problem. It seems I was right about that.

Berlin was a seedy, grimy place in those days, and I often socialised alone, as Juergen was antisocial and didn't want to catch anything. And this will surprise most people, he was not a party animal at all – actually he was quite reclusive and preferred his own company, certainly he preferred it to mine, in the end. Despite the druggy musicians and spaced-out artists hanging around, he was happiest with a cold shower, a cosy dressing gown and an early night alone in front of the mirror, putting lotion on his sad, blue face. Any research of local nightlife was done by me, alone in that Teutonic hellhole. Not that I'm bitter. My karmic aura prevents it. I'm just too angelic in the true sense of that word. I can direct healing energy with just a bat of my eyelashes. Capricorns though – they can be very difficult as they rarely do anything unless it has investment value – emotional or health wise and obviously financial. They don't really get the concept of living for the moment. As a cuspal Libran/Scorpio I'm more swayed by my impulses. I'm a mystical person – we only respond to deeper calls to our psyches.

"But going back to the spy rumours?

Well, you have to remember the international scene at that time. We had protests in Britain with the Greenham Common women, and the Cold War, things were very sensitive between the US and the USSR. There were quite a few British diplomats based in Berlin, and they often popped into the cleaners. It was a bit of a gossip spot, I suppose because historically it's always been a strategic place, between two empires if you like. In the 1980s, before the wall fell, there was still no formal, official contact between east and west Berlin – the two sectors were not allowed to interact. Unofficially of course there were negotiations going on all the time – West Berlin would be offered a person to bring over if they paid a "ransom" – for someone of interest, having the right skills or knowhow, it was an attractive proposition. The GDR would be pleased to get rid of them if it meant pulling some money in, they were virtually bankrupt, remember, and that way – if it was a high-ranking scientist, for example, they would avoid paying out someone's pension and save themselves some money. So, bartering went on, and it suited both sides … and we sometimes heard whispers of deals about to go down over the trouser press …

"But Maud, were you and Juergen involved in this horse trading?"

No, darling (**laughs**) – we were far too busy building our little empire. What would we know about international diplomacy and all that sort of thing?

"But your name has been linked previously with an ex-BBC security employee …"

Here the recording suddenly ended … (**It is with our deep regret this was to be Gabriel Morgan's last interview for *My Country Home* – he passed away suddenly in a road accident shortly after recording this. Investigations are ongoing**)

As told to the late Gabriel Morgan, *My Country Home* magazine, 2015

Capricorn Sun Sign cuttings

Capricorn

"I always had a need to be something more than human". So spoke the late David Bowie, entertainer to the cosmos and beyond. There's something about the mysterious sign of the goat that is always drawn to change, transformation and personal identity. More usually it comes in the form of chasing success, whether material, or professional, or both. Capricorns always have to get to the top of the mountain, even if it takes a lifetime, but to them it's always worth the slog and this is compensated with some desirable acquisitions along the way. They love living in the material world and enjoy being able to indulge their obsession for shopping. It's not just one, long, self-indulgent binge however; they're good at finding bargains and investments that benefit others. They're also kind hearted and make great mentors and teachers. Musical Capricorns, such as Mr Bowie, inspire young talents just beginning the long and treacherous climb to the summit; how to get there and how to keep their footing is always a valuable lesson.

Jolly Astrolly! Website, April 2016

Dear Readers,

How lovely for you to have me back amongst you, once again. I'll touch very briefly on the present planetary situation, and how it affects politics. The current planets are warning up for a noisy confrontation next January. There is a large conjunction in Capricorn between Pluto and Saturn early next year. A similar conjunction occurred in 1066 (October 14th if you're interested) when things didn't go terribly well for us on the south coast. Don't make any long-term commitments in the property, time-share or indeed atomic weaponry fields until spring 2020 has safely arrived. We hope.

Jolly Astrolly! Website, 2018

♏

C H A P T E R   7

Scorpio

London, 1992

In 1992 I had the dubious pleasure of being introduced to the writer, Apollo Lunt, celebrated author of "*Wainscotting*" and other literary works. We met at an awards dinner held in recognition of acts of bravery and selflessness by the general public – naturally neither of those applied to me, quite the contrary in fact, but I was happy to appear at the event and promote the Jollybottom brand. Apollo and I were on the same table with other celebrities of the era. I had wangled a seat next to him deliberately; his shocking debut novel about the squalid, brutal lives of artisan carpenters and joiners in the west country had sent him to the top of the Best Seller lists that year. Rumours were circulating of a film version of *Wainscotting*, with Quentin Tarantino directing. Even in Clenching, my modest Cotswold hometown, he was famous; the local Women's Institute had produced Moon-shot Marmalade in his honour. To this day they believed with a name like Apollo he had to be an astronaut, albeit with a filthy mouth and a ponytail.

Before writing "*Wainscotting*" he had of course dipped his quill into romantic novels using the pseudonym *Brandon Thrust*. It was the

80s Poll Tax riots that had triggered *Thrust* out of the Mills and Boon boudoir, and straight into The New Statesman. Using his real name of Apollo, Lunt had written a couple of plays, (*Down and Out in Guildford*, the *Weybridge Riots*, notably performed at the Royal Court) and a short novella packed with depravity based on life in a garden centre cafe, (*Buns and Roses*, Radio 4's Book at Bedtime). On the strength of this he was now feted and celebrated throughout the cultural landscape of the UK and beyond. I had plans to put Clenching (and myself) firmly on the cultural map and hoped to launch our own Literary Festival[1] that September. Having Mr Lunt as our VIP author would be a massive feather in my cap, if I could pull it off.

I researched my quarry carefully, as always. I knew he was a Scorpio, and therefore drawn to the darker side of life. And, true to stereotype, he was dark featured, almost saturnine in appearance, with his ink black hair pulled back in a ponytail. He was stocky, muscular from years of manual work, and he looked younger than his alleged 50 years. He gave different versions of his birthdate and birthplace, according to who was interviewing. A former "nit nurse" at his primary school claimed he had a mysterious "devil's" mark on the back of his neck that made the other children wary of him. A tabloid story hinted at his previous participation in alleged satanic rituals in Windsor Great Park. The story mysteriously sank before any photographs emerged – the "Palace", it was speculated, had intervened.

Between courses, and after several glasses of fizz, I engaged Apollo as best as I could on the imminent New Moon in his sign. There was also a nasty little celestial trine about to unleash from the heavens with a hint of conflagration and drama, but I promised him a more detailed reading if he would supply me with his actual time, and place of birth. He communicated using the least amount of speech possible and remained unsmiling, but he agreed to ask his mother about his arrival time. I was surprised to

---

[1] The Clenching Literary Festival finally took place in 2018. Mr Lunt declined his invitation to attend. We had a Love Island finalist as the Writer Guest of Honour instead.

discover his mother was still around, considering the lurid tales Apollo had woven about his birth and upbringing (found in a ditch as a baby, raised by wolves in Ilfracombe, etc). It seemed Mrs Lunt was still alive and held several executive positions with various animal charities, devoting all her time to non-human creatures, great and small. His infancy had been a bit unconventional though. He and his sister Shergar had slept in kennels during summer, in winter they were allowed baskets by the fireside. Anyway, I thought his mother sounded interesting, unlike her dour, taciturn son. I was having trouble hearing him even though I positioned my head as beguilingly near to his as I could without actually crawling up his nose. He was very quietly spoken, with a slight West Country accent promising cream teas and vanilla fudge but delivered with a soupcon of battery acid. Although his reputation spoke of how women found him irresistible, I didn't personally see the attraction – only a swarthy little chap with an inflated ego, misnamed after a Roman God and who was responding far too slowly to my charm campaign.

The event was being held in a banqueting hall of a London hotel. It was being televised for later transmission, but apart from an initial photographic swoop around the tables, the cameras were all concentrated on the stage where the awards were being presented. The table where Apollo and I were seated was lit by an artfully arranged nest of tea lights, and I was squinting to see him clearly. I could have worn my glasses, but my vanity had got the better of me, once again. I also struggled to hear against the background murmur, and the whole situation and Apollo in particular was getting on my nerves.

Emboldened by alcohol, I asked if I could see his famous "devil" mark. I didn't know what to expect – a type of branding? Was it a sort of stamp like they put on eggs? Had he been given a best before date by the Prince of Darkness?

I never thought he would agree (not that I would let that stop me), so I was surprised when he lifted his ponytail with both hands from the back of his neck and lowered his head for my inspection. I was immediately out of my chair clutching a tea light for illumination. Of course, I moved a little too fast and wobbled slightly, and before I knew it a streak of flame was running up his ponytail. Apollo, God of Light, had caught fire. I was transfixed, horrified, and didn't know what to do. It turned out he could turn up the volume when necessary and his screams went through the sound barrier. There was suddenly a hush around us, and everyone focused on Apollo. Especially me. A waiter, passing nearby with an ice bucket, pulled out the bottle, threw the ice water over Apollo, and wrapped the back of his head in a soaked tea towel. Marvellously fast reaction. I made a mental note to have him nominated for a special award. The whole table stood watching in horror. People passed napkins to the heroic waiter as he gently mopped the now drenched head. My horror was now mixed with fascination as Apollo's hairline appeared to move as if on strings to unseen seismic tremors and came to rest over one eye. It seemed the trademark angry ponytail had lost its moorings, and its owner, was now sat down, spluttering, and possibly spitting, in my direction. Security, first aid people and an ambulance were called.

By a big bit of luck, the flames had been put out almost immediately, and he had not been seriously burned, although damage to the ponytail was irreversible. In a gesture almost theatrical Apollo pulled the soggy, champagned-flavoured toupee from his head. He was completely bald.

No one spoke for a few seconds. It wasn't the best moment to pick, but the Jollybottom motto has always been Fortune Favours the Brave so in a wobbly little voice I found myself asking, *"can I see that mark on your neck now please?"*

Scorpio Sun Sign cuttings

MUSICAL SCORPIO

Often they're not as terrifying as people fear them to be. Sometimes the Scorpion temper is buried well underground, alongside a few disturbing sexual fantasies perhaps, but safely out of the public domain. If you dare to mislead them however, or trip up in the telling of your side of the story, well, let's all just hope back in 1982 or 83 or 84, little baby Kim Jong-Un wasn't born under Scorpio. They do have loads of intuition and an almost supernatural feel for what works and what doesn't. Sexuality is at the heart of their inner being, yet this message often comes across, particularly with female vocalists, in indirect and subtle ways. Think Joni Mitchell and Diana Krall. Proof, if proof were needed that Scorpios can be one classy act.

When considering Scorpios, think Cancer, think Pisces, and then think a lot, lot worse. One hardly needs to imagine the scenario created when a hapless swimmer in the cross currents of life finds himself unwittingly embracing an unobserved jellyfish, lurking in shallow waters. Sadly, where Scorpios are concerned, darkness and venom are all too familiar companions of this unpleasant type of water sign. Also, often sexually deranged, but kind to animals and firm eco-warriors.

Most serial killers can be found under the sign of Scorpio, which gives some indication of their special attributes. They're not a sign that enjoys being a team player, needing solitude, stealth and concentration for activities such as hunting and shooting. They do well when expending all their energy and are suited to the multiple challenges of the pentathlon. They also take to potholing, probably a little too much than is good for them. If you live with a Scorpio try and keep them above ground, and never buy a house with a cellar. Or turn your back. Or turn the light off. Ever.

Riffin' with Maud, The Riff Magazine, May 2019

♋

CHAPTER 8

Cancer

Little Clumping, Glos. 1997

In 1997 the word on the street in Clenching, the undisputed hub of rumour and gossip, was that Celebrity Chef and TV personality Monique Hart had rented a local property. I'm not exaggerating at Clenching's reputation for information gathering – it's no coincidence the British government based their spy centre at GMCQ, just up the road from Clenching. It must be something in the Cotswolds' air. Monique, it was said, was looking to establish a new restaurant here. The property in mind was the Old Malthouse in Little Clumping, an isolated place about 5 miles from Upper Clenching. It seemed she and her husband were renting with a long-term plan to buying it and to develop the adjoining land into a vineyard.

I had bumped into Monique over the years and knew her slightly. We had both worked on the same sort of TV programmes when young, and she had done well in making a giant leap from junior runner with big hair and 80s attitude, to having her own cookery programmes as unique Monique, the hot-stuff Chef. Now in her fifties, like me, she was the doyenne of the British foodie scene. She was confident, engaging and very attractive – I like to think we still had a lot in common. Of course, she was born under the sign of Cancer, with Leo rising, so her best moments in front of the camera were of her in her kitchen, domestic goddess-like with a welcoming hearth and home to entrance the viewer inside. She was charismatic with her long red hair swept into a romantic chignon, and, tendrils loosening in the steamy kitchen, she stirred the sauces, and some basic instincts, of plenty of viewers. She radiated heat and wielded a blowtorch on a *creme brulee* like a sultry dragon. Men were simultaneously terrified and besotted with her.

Her personal life had been a bit tumultuous but really, whose hasn't? Those of us destined to shine brightly in the dark skies of life, are made indestructible by the tempering of experience. Or at least that's what I came up with when I was asked to write the preface, as one of her "dearest, oldest friends" to her first book, "*Summer Memories with Monique*". On the cover she was wrapping her tongue around a cherry in a rather saucy – some may say risqué – manner. She went on to recreate this by wrapping her tongue around a mince pie for "*Christmas Memories with Monique*" – the summer barbeque book "*Sausage Memories with Monique*" was still with the lawyers.

Monique shared her business operation with her current husband, Xavier. She pronounced his name as if she was bringing up a fur ball, and it made people anxious she had a tissue handy. I bumped into her in Clenching High Street not long after the golden couple had arrived in town. She and Xavier were out shopping, and we chatted about the recent General Election. There was a mood of optimism with a youngish, new Prime Minister in office, and the country seemed on the brink of creative change and innovation. Things could only get better …

"*Maud, sweetie! – what are you doing here???*"

"*Monique, how lovely – I heard you were in town. Have you settled in?*"

She gave a lacklustre laugh, whilst Xavier pulled a face.

"Well, we've *got plumbing problems, builder problems- honestly Maud, it's never ending … but our landlord has promised us he'll get it sorted …*"

She smiled one of her mega-watt smiles, and Xavier made a little Spanish "what can you do ?" gesture in the background.

"Our stuff should arrive from Spain soon – promise me you'll come to dinner when you can?"

So, our sort-of-friendship over the years entered a new phase. We were to be neighbours, and I would put the past behind me. Although …

… sometimes one can't help carrying a little niggle of hurt in one's heart, however good natured and forgiving I always aim to be. I couldn't shake off a memory that went back to the 1980s when I was ambitiously working towards a TV job and came up against Monique as a rival.

In fact, a TV producer, Gideon Weitz, had auditioned us both for the same job on a daytime show. It was to be a jokey, brief cookery piece, where I or another would cook a recipe donated by someone famous – *"A Dish du Jour"* if you will. The donor could be anyone in the public eye so long as the recipe was simple, and the calibre of the celebrity was usually simple too. Inevitably this meant a boy band singer or a soap opera actor, but occasionally it was a politician and once, famously, a contribution from a bishop – *"A Dish from a Bish"*.[1] Of course, the whole thing was non-sense and entirely made up by the Production Team, and notably *Skylark Hemmings* who played Gail Swinefever, (the promiscuous yet caring slut of a veterinary nurse from *The Furry Infirmary*), had never eaten *"Granny Hemming's apple baked cod fillets"* in her life, let alone cooked them, but pulled in the most plaudits from the public.

Rewind to a few months back before this audition, to an evening when Monique and I had found ourselves at the same dinner party. The conversation had turned to old family recipes, and I mesmerised everyone with my story of *"Jollybottom's Swiss Geschnetzeltes"*, a family favourite my grandfather had entertained us with. Before eating this veal dish, we were all required to give a yodelling demonstration, to open the lungs up and brace the stomach, ready for the incoming alpine feast. It was, of course,

---

[1]   *A Dish from a Bish* turned out to be *Abbott's Pudding*, a Portuguese recipe the archbishop had picked up during his time as a Club 18-30 host on the Algarve.

     Grandpa may have enjoyed sharing the Swiss Dish story, but he certainly never cooked it, or to my knowledge ever set foot in a kitchen, unless it was to chase a domestic servant into the scullery.

quite mad, and most likely my dear grandpa, as a consummate liar and confidence trickster, had never been to Switzerland in his life, let alone been the war hero hiding in Heidi's hay loft he often told us about. Still, the yodelling was fun even if Quentin[2]over did it. Once the yodelling over, we were allowed to tuck in.

On the day of the audition, I was late getting to the studios in west London. I calmed myself while I waited for the person before me to do their stuff. I didn't know who was in the rehearsal room until Monique stepped out, smiled a sweet hello in surprise at seeing me, and told me Gideon was ready for the next person. As I look back at that moment, do I remember being a teeny bit puzzled at the way she seemed, i.e., *smug with victory*? Or has the passage of years brought an unpleasant tinge to my memory?

I did my best. I was experienced in doing pieces to camera and followed Gideon's direction as naturally as I could – naturally as in completely posed and rehearsed. This opportunity had been a long time coming and I'd spent years making myself ready. All went well until he asked me if I could tell a little anecdote about a favourite eating experience, perhaps, or a family mealtime memory? Just to gauge how easily viewers would relate to my chatty personality. I steeled myself with Jollybottom self-assurance as I sailed into my *Geschnetzeltes mit Yodel* experience but was perplexed to see Gideon suddenly frowning and telling me to stop.

You may have guessed the rest, dear reader … It seemed Monique had told the very same anecdote, just a little while before me, and had completed her audition with a heart-warming yodel to clinch it.

I was furious. That treacherous, conniving crab had pinched my story with her pincers. No-one remembers a slight like Maud …

So, here we were, years later in 1997, friends again and looking forward to spending time with each other. My brother Quentin and I were to enjoy an exquisite supper at Monique and Xavier's new home, and

---

[2]   Quentin always overdoes everything, including yodelling, and this self-centred display at 6 years old, was only the beginning. Of course, he was violently sick afterwards.

the place certainly did have great potential for their plans. Quentin, a confirmed bachelor as the old convention had it, had by now long abandoned his plans for a ballet career, and was earning a living as a bespoke carpenter and joiner. He hadn't met Monique before, but they'd hit it off immediately, and he was shamelessly ingratiating himself with her handsome husband. I hoped this wouldn't lead to any Quentin type problems. We were both enjoying a tour of the property when in my head, a shrill sounding bell from my past suddenly rang. As my eyes travelled over the various items of artwork, framed pictures and bits and pieces on a sitting room windowsill, I spotted a small, abstract shaped piece of glass on the shelf. It was an award, mounted with a label declaring *"Best Newcomer to Day Time TV 1983"*. From somewhere, deep down inside my soul, a blood curdling noise was trying to escape out of my mouth. It was the sound of a strangulated yodel. I suppressed it into a strange coughing sound as my eyes swam in a reddish haze. I sat down for a moment while I recovered my equilibrium and dug deep to produce my perfect-for-daytime TV artificial smile. Monique paused for a moment and stared at my sudden attack of "hay fever", but soon continued with her commentary. The moment passed and the rest of the evening was an uneventful success.

Quentin is always good company with his never-ending supply of scurrilous celebrity gossip – sometimes it even has a grain of truth about it. I knew the couple liked him and were happy to entrust him with some remedial carpentry work in their cellar where a lot of their stuff, transported from Spain, was now stored. Monique was keen to get this done – the landlord had given his permission, and the property was desperately short of storage. The couple were going back to Spain for a quick business visit, so it appeared an ideal time for Quentin to get busy with his toolbox and fix some cupboards. She gave me a spare pair of keys to the Old Malthouse for when they were away. I promised to look after them, keep an eye on things (and Quentin) and perhaps do a good luck blessing ritual on the property? Monique squealed with delight at the very suggestion. It was time to do my research.

I like to give hand-made gifts when I can. Although I had taken flowers with me to Monique's, I really intended to give her some sort of new home, good fortune keepsake, the sort of thing I love to make from my own original, esoteric designs. I did have a ready supply of my special little fortune bags that could be adapted for each occasion as appropriate. Quentin planned to be back at the Old Malthouse in 2 days, so I would accompany him with my good luck tokens and distribute them around the place.

I draw the line at doing spells – I'm not a witch, despite what some say about my uncanny "special" powers – but I like to give a person, a possession and/or a property a special "Maud" blessing and exercise my talents occasionally. My little feng shui fortune bags are tiny, made of red, silk-looking material and designed to be hidden in secret places. In the old days Sparky[3], our in-house dressmaker and domestic help used to make them for me, but of course had since gone on to start her own fashion business, having some success with it. More recently Krystal had whiled away her time in various rehab clinics by sewing these unique little bags, and I sourced all sorts of lucky gems, and herbs, to fill them with. The trick was assembling the right mixture – in the wrong hands a Maud amulet could become a "curse purse". I thought a long while deciding on Monique's mixture.

Three days later Quentin and I were unlocking the front door of the Old Malthouse. He was aiming straight for the cellar as planned, and I would be wafting around the upper floors, smudging some sage, and hiding my little bags. Judging by the looks exchanged between Xavier and Quentin I thought the master bedroom would soon need some good fortune, so I wedged one of the little bags behind an ancient oak dressing table. I put a couple of others around the room including one behind a radiator and was working my way through the other rooms when I heard Quentin yelling my name. I made my way down the steep cellar stairs and was shocked to see the basement floor flooded with water. All sorts of things were floating around and Quentin, with bare feet and rolled up

---

[3]   Sparky, or Electra as I believe she now calls herself, runs a little shop on South Molton Street, Mayfair, London. Some patronage from the Jollybottoms in the early days helped set her on course, but she rarely acknowledges this in public.

trouser legs was trying to grab them from his vantage point on an upturned wooden case. Some wine bottles had rolled out and were bobbing along in front of us – I grabbed the nearest. The water wasn't more than five or six inches deep but enough to do considerable damage. I made my way upstairs to phone for help, leaving Quentin masterminding his rescue operation.

It took some weeks for the flood insurance to come through. That first week of June had seen freakish amounts of rain and half the country was submerged. Monique and Xavier had returned from Spain immediately and, although she never raised it with me, I began to suspect Monique thought it was my fault the flooding happened. I couldn't imagine why – why would I do such a thing? Perhaps her guilty conscience made her see things this way? Obviously, her own shabby behaviour years ago still cast a dark shadow on her psyche. I, personally, prefer to cast off any negativity in my soul's striving for purity and perfection.

That summer was wet, miserable, and by the end of August, catastrophic. Life at the Old Rectory went on however, and I busied myself in various local events. I heard less and less from Monique, and it was only by a chance conversation in the butchers in October I found out they had abandoned their plans for the Old Malthouse and had disappeared abroad. There was, it seemed, quite a bit of gossip about their sudden departure. Questions had been raised about their previous success in Catalonia and Xavier's integrity as a wine producer was in doubt. Indeed, the bottle I brought home with me on the day of the flood was a little puzzling. It had been one of their own products as the beautifully designed label of two little crabs[4] on a Spanish beach, would testify. How strange then that the water damage had caused the label to peel, revealing a Spanish supermarket budget label underneath? I showed our local wine merchant the bottle and soon all his colleagues in the area had made the same discovery with their stock.

---

[4]   The label was designed in 1995 and featured two crabs, one with curly red hair like Monique's. If I describe it as less van Gogh and more Sponge Bob Square Pants aesthetically, I think you'll get the picture.

The most intriguing whispers about Monique and Xavier concerned the Old Malthouse. Long after the flood insurance issue had been sorted local cleaners were brought in, and particularly tasked with eradicating the lingering smell permeating the main bedroom and living quarters. The place was scrubbed and scoured for days but the smell persisted, and when the central heating was switched on to help dry the place, it became like a tropical breeze downwind of Billingsgate fish market. The place stank.

In my experience karma can be swift and decisive, but usually it takes its own sweet time. Sometimes, speaking as someone with special powers in these realms, I like to help karma along. My little red feng shui bags always have a filling unique to their owner, but I'd never used frozen prawns before …

Cancer Sun Sign cutting

Sporty Cancer

Another water sign, Cancer the crab is drawn to the ocean in the form of sailing, canoeing and deep sea diving. They are however keen to try most sports, despite their reputation for being bad losers, long-standing grudge bearing and taking any form of stimulant available. Although prone to giving opponents the notorious cancer-the-crab death stare, they can be surprisingly supportive to fellow team members, especially when mentoring novices. Many celebrity footballers are found under Cancer, and often many women are found under celebrity footballers.

Jolly Astrolly! Website, April 2016

Jupiter, the lucky planet, is keeping tabs on your sign but you will also feel the influence of Mercury, and we all know that means trouble. Don't make any impulsive career decisions and do have your immigration status clarified. Venus arrives in May, thankfully bringing with it a beautifying influence. Your appearance is long overdue for a make-over. That "all day spent on the allotment" look has had its day. The appearance of the Super Moon, or Blood Moon as it is known to the werewolf fraternity Cancer mixes with, finds people under the Crab (or in some cases, with crabs) strangely disturbed. Always prey to odd mood swings allied to the tides, the aberrant nature of this week's lunar events will be enough to send Cancerians completely off their – think Bates' Motel in "Psycho" – rockers. If you are a neighbour of the above a city break somewhere with high security is recommended.

Arc Welding Weekly, April, 1993

MUSICAL CANCER

You'll soon recognise a Cancerian if you have the misfortune to get stuck in a lift with one. They're the type to engage you with descriptions of their latest digestive problems in graphic detail. If you're with one on tour, make sure they eat properly and their accommodation is comfortable, preferably with homely touches, if you want to draw their performing potential out from under their shell. If you are unlucky enough to get nipped by their pincers, be prepared to hear of every mistake, misdemeanour and mess up you ever made in their company as they can hold a grudge to Olympic standard and beyond. They're a bit of mishmash personality wise; intrepid sailors who can't wait to make the voyage home, but also protective she-cats who can freeze out personal space invaders with one withering look or sharp remark. Either way a potential nightmare, but oddly they work well within the group dynamic and are sensitive to others. They don't hog the limelight, they don't deliberately outshine the rest of the band, and if you all learn to step sideways and avoid upsetting them, they do make beautiful music.

Riffin' with Maud, **From The Riff Magazine, September 2017**

Crabby Cancer

A conflicted sign, Cancer values his or her home life above everything, yet yearns to travel at the slightest glimpse of a duty-free outlet. Sensitive and emotionally guarded, they tend to come undone in the company of other water signs and can sometimes weep with Piscean intensity, and only slightly more sincerity. Often highly strung, although not quite on the neurotically upper register of Virgo, for example, they are very influenced by the moon's waxing and waning. This sometimes leads to them being taken in for questioning and social workers becoming involved. When engaged in unkind behaviour their preferred modus operandi is slinging barbed bullets of verbal spite to lacerate their victims. They make excellent foreign correspondents as they scuttle across the globe. Fleet Street once rattled to their collective pincer movement. Also good at picking just the right ISA to secure their homecoming nest-egg.

Spotlight on Satanism magazine, July 1989

♌

CHAPTER 9

Leo

Harlow, Essex, 2000

I first met Xander Bride at a Royal Academy summer reception. Although he was one half of the successful architectural practice, Bride and Gallagher, his girlfriend Kiko was more notorious with the paparazzi and celebrity watchers of the time. Looking the archetypal architectural type – black undertaker clothes, horn rimmed glasses and an intense, sober gaze, he was colourfully outshone and outvoiced by Kiko, an avant-garde performance artist. She was a completely different platter of sushi to Xander; noisy, overpowering and literally falling over herself to grab attention.

Her performance "events" involved throwing herself operatically out of windows, dangling off balconies, and popping up out of chimneys. All done, up to now, in complete silence and with a very straight face. Think Yoko Ono crossed with Buster Keaton. The approaching millennium however, had caused her to suddenly start screaming incoherently at the climax of the piece. Like millenarian sects in history, the big change approaching in the calendar precipitated weird and disturbing behaviour – even weirder in Kiko's case. Her vocalised anguish was hard to interpret – most already had a headache by then – but she claimed they were adopted Samurai Warrior screams. Protests screamed at the social constraints that were crushing humankind, mainly by the built environment. Odd then, that she chose to hook up with an architect and designer of the said built environment, but perhaps she was the ying to his yang. Of course, she was completely off her head and likely to literally lose it, sooner or later.

Kiko's origins were steeped in oriental mystery. She was believed to have a Japanese mother and English father and had arrived at Goldsmiths[1] via Andover in Hampshire. Not a stranger to myth creation myself, I admired her talent for self-promotion in the face of complete absence of talent. I'd worked for years with various pop stars by the Year 2000 – when Xander asked me to help Kiko with a special project I thought it would be a piece of cake. Kiko loved to perpetuate the myth she was a reincarnated Japanese monkey spirit – she told me this at our first meeting when I agreed to act as her astrological consultant. She was a crazy, exhibitionist Leo with Aquarius for a rising sign. Always pioneering the latest ideas and concepts in the loudest, most attention seeking way possible. Quite a handful for the intense, zipped up man-in-black Xander, born under Virgo. Ten years of life with Kiko had prematurely aged the man. Ten years of life with Xander had driven Kiko to crazy land and out the other side. But opposites attract, and added to this *folie a deux*, was piggy-in-the-middle Simon Gallagher, Xander's partner, who had patiently been carrying a never to be extinguished multi watt torch, for Xander. Simon lived for the special day Kiko eventually hit the ground and stayed there – the sun may also rise but with any luck Kiko wouldn't, or so he hoped.

Her unique party piece consisted of her dangling her upper body over various windowsills as a pair of her studio minions would hold one of her – it must be said – large feet to stop her completely falling. Sometimes we saw Kiko hanging upside down from her waist, and other times she hung more dramatically almost completely vertically but with firm wrists shown wrapped around her ankles. The recent performances were now

---

[1]   Goldsmiths – 1988 – YBAs

accompanied with blood curdling screams. It had certainly livened up a quiet day at Lords' cricket ground recently. On an unknowable acoustic level, she must have been devastating – keepers at nearby London Zoo reported animals with hearing loss for weeks afterwards.

Xander Bride had met Kiko at a reception for YBAs, Young British Artists, about ten years previously. He seemed to despise her/tolerate her/ worship the ground she seemed desperate to throw herself towards in a never-ending cycle of torment. He martyred himself with depressing regularity as she embarrassed/humiliated/showered him with affection – all in all a typical Virgo/Leo relationship. He wallowed in self-loathing every time she surpassed herself in histrionics. She kept popping up out of chimneys on castles and drooping over balconies, and the larger the structure, the more dramatic the event. Legal issues with Battersea Power station were still ongoing. Her fascination with new buildings – a touch of the Aquarius rising sign – made her plan new events at bigger, scarier structures. I wasn't sure how she had contributed to Bride and Gallagher's winning bid to build a new Millennium Library. Perhaps the organisers hadn't heard of her or were unaware of her connection to the practice. Or perhaps they had heard of her, and thought she might lend a bit of edgy arty credibility to the project? Stuck as the building was, outside of the M25 in a dreary "new town" plot, its attractions weren't glaringly obvious.

On this bright sunny April day, the great and the good had gathered to see the unveiling of the new municipal library. There was a new, low rise square building with wide glass windows and a central atrium, but they'd also renovated a tower – incongruous next to the modern build but listed from a previous existence as part of a Town Hall, and too important to the local residents to decommission. Now used as a storage/reference library archive, Kiko had chosen this place for her "performance". The mayor was here milling amongst the plebs, a brass band were tuning up, and some local girl guides and scouts were half-heartedly practising a drill sequence. The public and local press were allowed some access before the actual unveiling ceremony. They wandered bemused into the shiny, new building – the press in particular hoping to be on the scent of a wasted council tax controversy. Some local primary schools had been closed for the afternoon so there was also a sprinkling of young families attending. A reception of canapes and drinks was available to ticket holders in the new "Interaction Zone", and I noticed the council workers taking every opportunity of refilling and refuelling, making me loathe the general public with a renewed ferocity I hadn't felt for years – since the last Clenching Town Fete, in fact …

But today was a very different affair. I was here professionally as Kiko's CA, or Celestial Advisor. I had picked this date with great care, acting on my own instincts and with careful surveillance of the heavens. The council officials and other lesser bodies did not agree with my choice, citing it as Hitler's Birthday amongst other things, but I insisted as I had every right to do, because only I could predict when the stars were at their most benign. The heavens and I communicated in our unique way, as always.

The tension built as the clock ticked towards 2.00pm. I had met with Bride and Gallagher in the reception area, and we had oozed and schmoozed graciously with the VIPs. In fact, I had been a little concerned at Simon Gallagher's enthusiasm for the white wine (served out of *boxes* – how very "New Town") a couple of hours previously. I took Xander aside and told him to keep an eye on his partner. Xander reassured me Simon would take a quick nap in the upstairs "Interfactual Zone" (Reference Library) before the unveiling. Kiko was completely absent as she prepared herself somewhere private where monkey spirits go before big events. I'd counselled her to isolate herself before the unveiling to avoid tension and she had taken this advice on board. One had to be thankful for small mercies.

We gathered outside the building for the speeches. The mayor, who looked about fourteen and who had really wanted a new skateboard park rather than a library, managed to puff up his own metaphorical tyres in his vote of thanks to all concerned. Xander looked mildly pleased and attempted a shy smile which, under his sunglasses, looked sightly sinister. I couldn't see Simon anywhere. The other worker bees (all wearing architectural black) in the practice seemed pleased with the final outcome of all their hard work during this long, extensive project. In fact, the new building looked amazing in the spring sunshine. One wall had been covered in a deep purple wrapping, and it was from under here, from one of the upper windows, Kiko was to make her "statement". The public stared up at the wall, and all went quiet.

The mayor was just getting to the "it gives me great pleasure to declare the new Millennium Library open …" part as the drapery was pulled away, and the main wall of the building was exposed. A hideous sound of wounded pain and terror – just the ticket for a family occasion – rumbled up and out of the highest window, closely followed by Kiko as she threw herself over the windowsill and downwards, until her body dangled operatically, pointing towards the floor.

Then, just as dramatically, another human body threw themselves out of a different window, also screaming. Everyone gaped in collective horror. The second body turned out to be Simon Gallagher who had clearly not had the nap he should have done. The crowd tensed, too scared to move in case it propelled him down. Obviously an amateur in the dangling stakes, he was out of the window by two arms and one leg, and edging, and screaming, towards the ground. He was screaming protestations of love for Xander, who anxiously twitched an eyebrow to show how disturbing this was. Meanwhile Kiko paused for a second with the samurai stuff and turned her head awkwardly to see what was going on. It was obvious her inner monkey spirit was riled in annoyance as she sensed the crowd's – *her* crowd's – waning attention at her performance. She started yelling again, louder than Simon who was still bewailing Xander with unrequited love. Simon upped his game and went for even louder wailing. The crowd were both bewildered and deafened. Simon looked about to leave his window at any moment. The St John's Ambulance people drew close and produced a blanket from somewhere. The mayor was struck speechless and then a Girl Guide suddenly started screaming as Simon fell – dangled – fell a bit more – and dangled a bit more as we saw that one of his socks – premium cotton argyle from Harvey Nichols – had caught by a whisker on the window frame. I noted one of the junior architects noting this in a pocketbook – no doubt a snagging list. Kiko was looking thunderous, and sounding it, as Simon stole the show from under her nose and dangled more precariously than she did. There was a loud gasp from the crowd as the heroic woollen thread eventually gave way. Simon fell into the blanket and Kiko stopped screaming, incensed. The crowd, shaken and unsure what to do next, murmured quietly and shyly started to leave. Meanwhile Kiko was still dangling so someone called the Fire Brigade to get her down. They arrived within minutes and after heaving Kiko over a manly shoulder she was taken away. Away to somewhere soothing where unhappy monkey spirits go to heal. Andover possibly?

I took a clear message away from this occasion. Always keep Leos and drunk architects away from crowds and open windows. It's best to leave them alone in dark places while they dream their days away of bright, shiny futures.

Leo Press Cuttings

All Leo infants should come with a warning – allow him or her to take centre stage and show off, and you may as well surrender your British passport here and now. Showing off is something foreigners are good at, and rather noisy about doing, but it is simply nothing one of us should aspire to. A junior Leo must be forcibly restrained from climbing on stage and performing – whether in the classroom, on the stage or, often, in the witness box. They cultivate the adoration of an audience and will stop at nothing to secure their place in the spotlight. Known for their hideously cheap jewellery and sun worshipping proclivities they are often found roaming in packs on Mediterranean promenades. The sonic intensity of their collective braying sounds is recorded as causing tectonic plate displacement.

Those born under the sign of Leo must find a sport they excel in, as they are never satisfied with an average performance. Being overlooked is a continual nightmare for these self-obsessed creatures. Activities such as high-powered racquet games and motor sports are attractive to Leos. Formula One racing is the ultimate Leo high risk activity, with plenty of room on the winners' podium for their enormous heads to dominate. Leos make fascinating and attractive sports heroes, but a Leo child is usually unbearable. Try to avoid having one, if possible.

The Spectator, November 1998

MUSICAL LEO

This is the year when your dreams of becoming a Country and Western star may take off, but you must insist on the widest brim on your Stetson. Try not to let your natural personality trait of megalomania interfere with others in the recording studio and make the most of Jupiter's lucky bounty when it moves forward on April 8th. It leaves again in August, and it's likely your reputation will nosedive into obscurity once again. Aim for Nashville but settle for Luton.

From *The Riff* Magazine, September 2018

♈

CHAPTER 10

Aries

Monterey, California 2009

"It happened in Monterey, a long time ago …"

It happened in Monterey, in 2009, so not as far back as Mr Sinatra's[1] song would have us believe.

I was 68 and my sister a little younger. Together we were fighting an unlikely public crusade against ageing – easier by day when plastered with make-up and styled to perfection but not so easy in those unguarded moments when we caught ourselves in the mirror, unprepared and camera unready. We felt obliged to mouth the trendy platitudes about the positive aspects of ageing – it was an essential vibe in today's world, and I wasn't ready to disappoint our followers. Together, Krystal and I encouraged our older followers in retaining what was left of their youth and beauty. It wasn't in our contracts but the obligation towards our commercial partners and sponsors was always there. Of course, when I say *our*, I really mean *my*

---

[1] *"It Happened in Monterey"*.© Frank Sinatra, *Songs for Swingin' Lovers*. Capitol Records, 1956. Frank was one of Maud's clients, who sought her advice about his relationship with Mia Farrow.

followers, unless you include some deluded dog lovers from Krystal's end-of-the-pier show days. They still sent her fan letters signed with paw prints, poor souls. I had not had the substance abuse problems dear Krystal's life had been blighted with, and thanks to a lifetime of healthy intake and self-preservation, had so far escaped reasonably unblemished. I received fan letters telling me how wonderful I still looked – how could I argue with my public?

We were both staying at an exclusive spa-type holistic place in Big Sur, in Monterey County, a couple of miles off the Pacific Highway. The Golden Squaw Spa promised an enhanced Circle of Life experience, which it certainly lived up to in unforeseen ways. I had been engaged to speak at the Monterey Sea Spirit Festival and wanted to prepare holistically for the gig, which was to take place at the Monterey Aquarium. I also wanted to take advantage of the big discounts being offered from so many promoters and businesses connected to the festival, such as the Golden Squaw Spa. A 40% discounted top to tail *El Greco*[2] massage with camel dung compresses and free-range whelk oil was not to be sneezed at – actually, it turned out this *was* to be sneezed at in a certain heat, so we were both heavily dosed up with antihistamine. I was sent a complimentary ticket for myself and plus one, so Krystal and I booked in for a few days R&R prior to my engagement and to make the most of the Californian sunshine.

The spa resort was in a beautiful location, just a couple of miles from the Pacific Highway. The place had previously been a ranch, and the main treatment rooms, communal and office areas were grouped in low height, rustic style buildings with luxurious cabins spread out like satellites around them. All the pathways were framed with beautiful shrubs and flowers, and the scent of Californian poppies hung in the air. There was deep, deep silence, apart from birdsong and the gentle melody of wind chimes. It was idyllic. And yet, there was just the slightest, strangest vibe about the place

---

[2]   El Greco massage involves both the masseuse and the client undertaking a bout of wrestling while simultaneously applying essential oils etc. On the pre-approval Olympic Sport Recognition list.

that made me a trifle uneasy. I couldn't identify it and thought maybe I was just too uptight from the long plane journey to relax into the place. But I would give it a try.

On our first day we joined in with all the "activities" the Golden Squaw Spa had to offer. After our special eyelid lifting treatment ("*blepharitic renewal*") we were invited to a chanting ceremony. Group chanting was known to lift and direct the consciousness into a different – lighter – dimension, so they told us, so we thought we'd give it a go. We were given special hoods to wear with eyeholes cut out for our updated peepers to look through, and we were encouraged to keep our sustainable fabric bathrobes on all the time. The hoods were apparently impregnated with essential oils and stuff to enhance our facial skin and hair – the bathrobes were made from a gentle linen fabric, all recycled, all allergen free and all weaved locally by a prisoner rehab programme in nearby Salinas.

Neither of us could really tell you what the chanting was all about. The easiest way of describing it was to say it was like an odd sort of military-style, line dancing movement with a lot of strange shouting thrown in. It wasn't easy to do gracefully in a flowing robe and a hood with tiny eyeholes. There was a lot of chanting of alleged Native American phrases, and leg movements on the same beat, and then one arm would be stretched out ahead, seemingly pointing to the middle distance. I was intrigued and amused by this military style two-step/knees-up/sing-song – it didn't make any sense or have any authenticity, but we had a good laugh afterwards and were ready for a nice, long swim in the *Beyond Infinity* pool.

There were long trails through the forest surrounding the place with one major trail leading to the ocean a few kilometres away. I had been running on and off for years. I found it centred me and calmed me and led my brain into the creative places necessary to stay fresh for my calling. And it *was* my calling to be a mediator between the stars in heaven, and the stars on earth. Not always stars on earth, of course. Some minor personages of uncertain origin had made their way onto my client list over the years, but my intention was to be all inclusive. If you can "*walk with kings nor lose the common touch*[3] All Jollybottoms learned this poem in childhood.

I was keen to get hiking in this beautiful place, but Krystal needed some persuading. She eventually agreed to try a short hike first. If we made an early start the next day, I assured her, before breakfast, she would enjoy the peace and harmony of the environment and we may even spot some wildlife. This appealed to the eternal animal lover in her and she eventually agreed.

The whole emphasis of the place was on inner and outer sanctity, and some strict notices in the cabins and office areas reinforced this. Guests were not encouraged to leave the sanctity of the spa for any reason unless they were on a trail. There was to be no alcohol consumption in any of the communal areas, or trails, and discouraged in the cabins. An emergency intervention could be made available if this proved too difficult for anyone. Smoking was absolutely forbidden, anywhere, and anyone caught smoking would be asked to leave. As well as being a filthy habit and not in keeping with the spa's healthy ideals, the area was prone to drought and always at risk of forest fire.

So, of course, after repeatedly knocking on Krystal's door early the next day, I was not pleased when she eventually opened it, still wearing pyjamas and with a lit cigarette in her hand. And looking only slightly awake. I wasn't sure if the cabins had smoke alarms and didn't want to take the risk. She pouted and rolled her eyes at me, saying she had to have her breakfast fag before doing anything strenuous. And then she had a good cough to seal it.

"*Well smoke it outside for god's sake before you set the alarm off*" I snapped.

She stumbled out on to the little timber-constructed, and highly flammable veranda. As if deliberately trying to irritate me further she pulled a small hipflask out of her pocket and took a swig.

"*You need a hot drink inside you before any of that …*" I pointed at the flask. She responded with more pouting.

———————————

[3] If – A poem by Rudyard Kipling. The writer and poet. Not the man selling cakes.

"I'll make you a coffee and then we need to get going" I told her sharply, although the morning was foggy, and it was ages before we'd feel the warmth of the sun.

She shrugged and mumbled something at me – I ignored her and made for the kettle and little sachets of beverages in her room. She took ages to drink her coffee and I forced myself to stay calm with her. In fact, she had recently had to have Clodagh[4], one of her poodles, put down, and was very upset by it. And being upset usually led Krystal straight to the bar. I hadn't realised how upset she was until I overheard her speaking to someone in the airport about it. Her poor little voice trembled as I heard her say *"… you just have to do the kindest thing for them, and put them out of their misery …"* I'd become quite emotional, remembering how I had felt when my first little Shih Tzu, *Mosely*, went for his final walkies over the rainbow bridge. I'd had a succession of *Moseleys* since then – I found I couldn't adjust to any other name. When we had checked in to the spa, Krystal had also brought the reception manager, Enriquez, up to date about Clodagh. The two had bonded when it turned out he was also a dog lover and had dreams of showing at Crufts one day.

"Here you are, get this down you..." I passed her the drink. She looked a bit shaky and gave me her cigarette to hold, while she held the coffee cup with both hands. I was just about to ask her where and how she had got hold of the booze when the sound of footsteps through the bushes made us both turn, and a man suddenly appeared out of nowhere, with a camera aimed at both of us.

He was a short, sweaty little man with a familiar face breaking into a big smile as he came upon us, myself with a cigarette and Krystal with a hangover. Breaking every protocol in the Golden Squaw Spa rule book. Our visitor was Gordon Sax, celebrity stalker and muckraker photojournalist, notoriously employed by every seedy tabloid in the UK. *Greedy Gordon*, my nemesis.

---

[4]   Clodagh – one of the poodles. Krystal always named her poodles after female singing stars of the 60s and 70s, including the male dogs, often leading to urination/ identity problems (with the dogs, not Krystal).

"'*The readers will love this! How are you Maud, long time no see! Krystal sweet'art! 'ow you doin?*" he said.

"*Gordon*", I replied, curtly. Krystal stared at him.

"*Lovely spot, innit? Going for a run, are you? You sure that's a good idea?* He said as he looked at Krystal. "*Only I'd like to have a little word with you both before you set off. I met up with your old pal, Electra recently ... we had a chat about the old days.*"

This only added to my feelings of deep anxiety. Electra, or Edith, or *Snarky Sparky* as we knew her, wouldn't have missed an opportunity to kick a Jollybottom into the gutter.

"*Let's catch up later, Gordon – where are you staying?*" I said, forcing myself to speak normally.

"*Right 'ere, Maud – I'm almost your neighbour! I've been 'ere a few days now and spotted you out and about. That's what I wanted to talk to you about, and show you the pictures I've got ...*"

My heart, already dropping, now hit the floor. The hike was cancelled. And so, I had a horrible feeling, was the rest of my career. I invited Gordon back to my cabin. I didn't want him inside Krystal's even though we were standing outside it; her untidiness and years of living in a giant poodle kennel had made her a bit lax in ways of hygiene etc. I didn't want this added to the list of Jollybottom shortcomings Gordon was itching to share with the world.

It only took him about 20 minutes to sum up his recent project with us in starring roles. He started by showing the secret video he'd made of us taking part in the chanting activity. He was more technically minded than I gave him credit for, as we watched ourselves marching up and down, robed up and wearing hoods and yelling collectively in perfect timing. The camera zoomed in on myself and Krystal stretching our arms straight ahead in perfect Nazi salutes. All as if choreographed by Leni Riefenstahl and set to happy cheerful German oompah band sounds – a soundtrack to murdering people and burning crosses. Gordon smirked as I felt my face freeze, knowing how he'd made us both look. Why us? Krystal looked at the screen of his tablet, dumbfounded. A little more enhanced than her usual state of dumbfounding. After the video he played an audio recording of Krystal speaking about poodle breeding – a snippet of the doggy chat she'd had with a stranger – was he? – in the airport lounge. "… *were just inferior, and really were better of out of it … makes for better breeding in the long run …*" Of course, she was talking about dodgy poodles, but in this febrile Nazi context it came across as her preference for selective human genocide. Just to round things off, Gordon played some audio of me next, saying "… *I don't think I've ever got over losing Mosely*". Newspaper headlines started flashing in my brain.

"*Ok Gordon. I see where you're going with this*" I said. "*Why bother telling us what you have in store exactly?*"

"*I don't want this to be made public, Maud*" he said in a wheedling voice. "*I'm happy to hear your side of the story, after all*". *I just want to help you, and Krystal, where I can …*" He spoke in a kindly tone as if he'd made a special trip to save us, instead of throwing us under the proverbial bus.

"*And how would you – or WHY would you help us?*" I said as I fought back the anger.

He stopped smirking, and suddenly spoke in a cool, efficient voice. "*I can stop this story getting out. I know you're speaking at the festival here – you don't want this splashed over the newspapers. I can help you if you help me…*"

And then he spoke – he said a man's name. The name of a man well known to the British public, and with a good reputation. As an ex-politician he was considered quite unique in this category. He had devoted many years since leaving government to helping good causes and charitable organisations. And he had consulted with me on several occasions for cosmic guidance. Specifically for guidance with his marriage, and how to deal with the relationship his wife was having with someone in the Royal Family. And now Greedy Gordon was on the trail of a full-blown British scandal, and we were being used as bait.

I didn't push him out of the cabin door, but I politely said I needed a little while to think about things, before responding to him. He smiled again, a big shark smile without a hint of warmth about it, and said he hoped to see us later at the spirit cleansing ceremony. Mentally, I wanted to cleanse his spirit with a gallon of petrol and a flaming torch, but I smiled nicely as I propelled him firmly out of the door. I had to do something, quickly, to get him off our backs. The Spirit Cleansing Ceremony – whatever the hell that was – loomed later. Resources were limited but, the old Jollybottom motto (well, one of them, anyway) *nils desperandum* came to mind. I had to find out more about this ceremony malarkey, and how I could get rid of ghastly Gordon. I gave Krystal a long, hard look. I would have to send her in to bat for us. I'd let her sleep her hangover off before apprising her of her mission. I prayed the helpful reception manager Enriquez was on duty today. Despite lacking so much in some areas of her life, Krystal had been amply compensated by nature in others. Time to get to work …

First, let me say I never share anything that has been revealed to me by a client, unless they want something leaked on purpose. The politician friend who Gordon was gunning for, had been a regular client of mine since being ousted from the Blair government a few years back. His job loss came as collateral damage when a financial scandal blew up a few years back. He wasn't directly implicated – not that it mattered much in politics, but it had all blown over now, and he had moved on to better things. He headed up a high-profile charity with royal patronage – connections which his wife had found irresistible. I found it difficult to counsel him. If any sign under the stars was prone to being deceived, lied to, cheated etc it was Taurus. They always see the good side, rarely the bad, and they should never enter politics. Often, they're just too distanced from the real world and too focused on how they will improve it, to see what's going on under their noses. It was often down to me, Maud, to sadly shine a light of clarity into the murk.

Many hours later that day, long after darkness had fallen, we found ourselves seated in one of the larger rustic style rooms at the spa's centre. A vast round table with chairs was in place at one end of the room, while the rest of us were seated theatre style ready to watch the proceedings by candlelight. Volunteers – and I'm assuming they all had volunteered – were seated around the table with a few individuals in ceremonial regalia at the table's centre. The regalia was an interesting mix of feathers, leather strappings, and wild headdresses. Imagine a group of Freemasons getting together to perform The Birdie Song by candlelight. I scrutinised the volunteers and felt relieved to spot Gordon's sweaty little face at the table. I was pleased to see he looked a little nervous, and I felt a teeny ounce of guilt he'd been persuaded to take part, when neither of us obviously weren't. It was good work by Enriquez.

At last, the ceremony got under way. There was plenty of drumming, plenty of chanting (with audience participation – we all knew the words by now, as I realised the previous session had been a rehearsal for this) and plenty of shamanic spirit cleansing, apparently. Although, as someone who deals with spiritual issues constantly in my communion with the heavens, this looked to me like straightforward drug taking dressed up as Native American shenanigans. One of the bird/leather people did a little dancing on the spot routine, before passing a plate around the volunteers. Each volunteer around the table took an offering and put it in their mouth. The chanting was loud by now, and the room was fuggy with burning sage. It was hard to breathe, and I was getting a headache. I wanted to leave but couldn't until … and then it happened. Gordon's head suddenly slumped forward onto the table, and dribble ran out of his mouth. It was too much to hope that he was dead, but I certainly cheered up when he looked unconscious. The planets were with us, after all …

We were woken a few hours later by the sound of helicopters overhead, and dogs barking furiously. I opened my cabin door to see lights whirring overhead, people dressed in body armour with torchlights combing the shrub areas, and the sound of commands being yelled through a megaphone. I called reception to find out what was happening. It seemed Ghastly Gordon was happening, having woken from his drug induced slumber he'd decided to run amok through the spa grounds, possibly armed. Guests at the spa were terrified and the Monterey County Police Department weren't taking any chances with their armed response. He was last seen in reception, according to Krystal via Enriquez, wearing a bandana, improvised army fatigues, and threatening death and destruction to all unless they stopped chanting. Enriquez was confused as to what the man was saying. He had trouble translating *"nonstopbludychantin in my'ed, fer fux's sake"* which irritated Gordon further, who pointed a weapon wrapped in a robe (allergen free, sustainable fabric) which was possibly just an umbrella, possibly not, and who then ran off into the deep, dark woods, screaming obscenities. How very *Rambo*, I thought, laughing to myself. Some Hollywood war movies came to mind, and I could almost hear the *Ride of the Valkyries* playing in my head, before I shut it down immediately, remembering recent events. The thing to remember about those born under Aries, is that they all carry traits of the warrior inside them – they all have an inner Rambo, dangerous when unleashed. I thought Gordon's editor would be interested to hear all about his roving reporter's adventures so I would make sure he did. I still had some media contacts.

Two days later I gave a terrific speech at the Sea Spirit Festival, even if I am blowing my own little trumpet, darlings. The Monterey Aquarium was a wonderful venue, and the whole picturesque town looked beautiful in the early fall sunshine. Krystal loved seeing the sea otters, and Enriquez obviously loved seeing Krystal – he came along too, having a few days leave with "workplace trauma". He had played a very helpful role in the Chanting Ceremony – helpful to us, at the time, although the place was closed months later citing illicit drug parties as the reason. The hunt for Gordon eventually scaled down, although there were occasional sightings of a maniac living off grid in the northern California backwoods. Like the yeti, he was assumed to be an apocryphal creature. It seemed he was still at large, out there somewhere. Somewhere a very long way from Clenching, with any luck.

Aries Sun Sign cuttings

Aries

The Sign of the Ram
March 21ˢᵗ – April 20ᵗʰ

Frankly these are despicable creatures. Known for their aggression, those born under the sign of Aries are notorious for their mood-swings, demanding behaviour, and volcanic tantrums. And that's just the nice ones. Generally, they are very impulsive and never react kindly to criticism of their methods or strategy. As their strategy and motivation is usually limited to self-promotion in all areas, it's never wise to explore this face to face with an Aries unless head-butting is one of your favourite pastimes. Kinder astrologers refer to their traits of ego mania and assault and battery as strengths, important in the formation of new enterprises and rallying the troops. This kind of wishy-washy waffle cuts no ice with Maud Jollybottom. It was this kind of talk that cost us an empire. Mind Maud's words – when it comes to Aries keep them securely tethered. And as for their significant others – we shall remember them in our prayers.

Jolly Astrolly! **Website, April 2016**

Always in a hurry, impatience triggers most Arian outbursts which are often spectacular and seismic in nature. Growing older is not something Aries comes easily to terms with, but even the loudest, proudest, down, and dirty rocker has to watch his dodgy hip sometime. Try to approach any new relationship with a Libran with uncharacteristic restraint this autumn. An Aries/Libran duet can be a beautiful thing but keep it within professional and decency boundaries. In fact, try to keep it zipped up all together Aries, males and females, before all hell breaks loose, and a big mess ensues that someone else is left to clean up. Usually, that someone else is a Virgo, who always comes along with a noisy mop and bucket plus a whiff of sanctity to make sure their Virgoan good deed doesn't go unnoticed.

Riffin' with Maud, **From The Riff Magazine, September 2018**

Ram Lamb Ding Dong!

... In a survey of UK midwives, a high percentage reported actual physical assault from emerging new-born Aries babies. In the worst scenario a black eye and split lip was recorded, despite the assailant being premature and weighing less than 5lb. It will come as no surprise that this baby, along with fellow combatants, was born under the sign of Aries. Don't bother wasting time putting them in day care or tumble tots etc – they thrive in boot camps or on military assault courses, even while still in nappies (industrial strength). Adult Aries, especially females, enjoy cage fighting and kick boxing, often leading to kick-drinking. Always let them win.

'Babytalk' magazine, October 1998

CHAPTER 11

Sagittarius

Schiphol Airport, Amsterdam, 2015

The BA airline lounge wasn't crowded, despite it being the day after a public holiday. I guessed most were continuing to London, like myself, but maybe some were enjoying a stopover before getting their connecting flights elsewhere. We were scattered around the lounge in singles and small groups, a few people on their phones, others chatting with a drink, all taking advantage of this peace and quiet oasis away from the busy airport. Apart from a small religious group in one corner – a nun with two priestly companions, everyone else looked like they were travelling on business, all working age and dressed similarly. The lounge had huge displays of tulips in various eye-catching spots scattered about – it was spring, the loveliest time to visit the Netherlands' and I'd enjoyed spending my brief Easter break here.

I noticed something odd happening to the departure screens. It was late afternoon, a busy time in a busy place, but the screens were showing flights being cancelled at every gate and the sound of announcements outside in the airport general areas had stopped. I had been half heartedly chatting to an American man seated near me, after he'd kindly offered to get me a coffee. I was pleased with his good manners – at my present age of 74 I felt covered with a cloak of invisibility, and it was nothing to do with a boy wizard. Sometimes people recognised me, as a long ago face from off the TV, but usually it was only when I gave my distinctive name the penny dropped. Then I got asked to tell them either what sign they were, or what the stars had in store for them. It seemed my courteous American man didn't recognise me, had never heard of me, and found the name amusing.

"*Say what?*" he said, incredulous. "*What was your name again?*". I repeated it for him.

"*Jollybottom*" he repeated slowly. "*that's one hell of a name*".

"*It was Norman, originally. It's derived from the French, jolie bol*", I explained. "*It means a beautiful round thing, like a bowl, or some sort of mound …*"

"*Like a nice ass?*" he interrupted, a smile starting up on his face. It was an American face, rugged and chunky – probably mid-Western. Not handsome, but masculine and attractive.

"*Not quite*" I answered primly, deducting points for his rudeness. He'd been doing well up to now.

"*And what is your final destination, Ms Jollybottom?*" he spoke in a drawl, teasing out the syllables.

"*London*" I answered, deciding against explaining Clenching to a foreigner.

I was just about to ask him the same question when suddenly, outside the lounge there was the sound of gunfire and muffled screaming. The departure screens, inside and out, all went to black. One of the men seated in the lounge got up and walked to the centre of the lounge. He moved fast and carried his holdall close to his body. He was wearing a heavy winter coat over a suit, and we all stared, unthinking. And then we all made a collective gasp when he pulled a gun out of his bag, and started addressing us, his bewildered audience.

"*Don't move – stay still and keep quiet!*"

"*Oh shit*" the American muttered.

"*The doors have locked, automatically – don't try to leave. Don't move, keep still and no one will be hurt, Inshallah*"

No one moved. All eyes were on the man with a gun. He was sweating and looked nervous, and with good reason we now realised, reappraising the oversized coat he was wearing. It was belted loosely, and most likely covered explosives. How had he got through the security checks? Maybe he hadn't, and worked at the airport somewhere, plotting and planning for just this moment. How many more of them were there, outside of these glass doors? The screaming had stopped almost as soon as it began, and there was an eerie silence out there. We did as we were told and sat quietly waiting, as the anxiety started to build. I looked around the lounge at the other passengers. There looked to be about 20 people or so, maybe less, and this included two members of staff both in the airline uniform. They both stood at the bar serving area looking helpless, as if trying to recall the training handbook for moments such as this.

After about fifteen minutes I found enough courage to gently reach into my bag. I was after my manicure kit – I didn't think a book would distract me – before remembering I didn't pack it due to airline security rules. The irony. I could smell the acrid sweat off him before I looked up to see him standing in front of me, pointing the weapon at my head. A wave of fear went through me, and I sensed, rather than felt, the other passengers recoil. He spoke loudly in, I guessed, Arabic, and gestured angrily at me with the gun. It wasn't the right reaction, or even a sensible one, but I was irritated by him and his aggression, so I snapped at him to speak English. In, even I must admit, a rather haughty manner. The room was deadly quiet. I tried to suppress my trembling, but my glasses were wobbling on the bridge of my nose. "*Please*", I added, in a humbler tone.

The gunman stared at me. And then he gave a short, unexpected laugh and strode back to his original vantage point. I felt relief wash over my bones even if it was misplaced. A slight murmur of nervous voices started up and my American spoke out of the corner of his mouth "*…respect, lady – that took some cojones…*" I had no idea what he was talking about.

We all jumped as a landline phone in the bar area suddenly trilled noisily. The two staff members, a young man and woman, both turned automatically to answer it, but the gunman yelled at them to stop, and strode towards them. I saw them both flinch as he seized the phone angrily and rattled off a tirade – again in Arabic – down the line. He ended the call by slamming the receiver down. I hoped the person on the other end didn't wonder if they'd called a wrong number and would try again.

"*I hope* – said the American – *if we get out of this ok, we get to meet again, Ms Jollybottom*".

I stared at him.

"*Look me up if you're ever in New York – come and meet the team and see how an American election campaign works. It's brutal but we're not armed to kill – not often anyway*".

I thanked him, and said I might do that, one day. One day that this maniac with a gun may permit us to see. And, out of habit and to his great amusement, I asked him when his birthday was. He was taken aback but answered "*November 27 – Now why do you need to know that?*". "*Sagittarius*" I replied, softly. "*I like to know who I'm dealing with*". He grasped my hand, and I felt him press a business card into my palm. I put it in my pocket as we all retreated into silence, sat still as stone and waited for something to happen next.

Something did happen about ten minutes later. An object – maybe a hammer – crashed through the glass wall nearest to where the gunman was standing. A man wielding the hammer kept striking the glass until he could scream loudly in through the broken glass hole to his fellow ter-rorist. It looked like information was being given. Our gunman nodded and seemingly acquiesced to the instructions. He paced a little and then, with an ear blasting yell of something reached into his coat. I closed my eyes and braced myself against the explosion. I felt my American friend do the same – we were sitting closely together by now – there was no time to pray, to collect one's thoughts, or any of the things expects to do in that situation. I just closed my eyes and waited …

The room went dark, instantly, and then bright sparks of light like fireworks lit up the lounge. It took me a few seconds to make sense of the scene, but instinctively I knew a bomb had not been detonated. Something had exploded but turning to look at our assassin my brain couldn't trust what my eyes were showing me. The gunman was lying on the floor, pinned down by two priests and with a nun point a gun at his head. From the way his coat was flung open, with loose wires trailing from some explosive contraption, someone had pulled off a miracle just in the nick of time.

And then the overriding memory is of confusion, being ushered quickly out of the lounge and into some other room, having paramedics check us over and cups of tea and strong Dutch coffee being offered around. Paperwork had to be completed, interviews with police had to be completed. All in a blur and a sense of time being sped up. Oddly, two separate things remained in my head from what I call the "rescue time". Firstly, the large vase of tulips had been upended in the chaos, and water lay trickling across a display stand. Secondly, and I wasn't sure for a long time afterwards, but I thought one of the priests, an older grey haired but active looking guy, caught my eye just after disarming the gunman, and before marching the gunman out. The plan to blow us to kingdom come had been synchronised with the outside assailants apparently, our protectors – whoever they were – had to wait until the split second it was about to go off outside before intervening inside the lounge. Why would a hot looking priest catch my eye in a half wink in the middle of all that? It had to have been a stress induced hallucination.

Eventually, upsetting though it was, we were released and allowed to travel the next day and complete our journeys. I tried not to relive the memory as I sat, once again, waiting for my Heathrow flight to be called.

There were two happy outcomes to the experience further down the line. A few days later, back in Clenching, I received a beautiful bouquet of spring flowers – all colours of tulips mixed in with roses and calla lilies. There was a note with them with just a few words, "…*from your favourite priest, Adam*". Adam! Yes, of course it was, I knew that priest looked familiar. My mysterious Adam, who once apparently worked at the BBC but was more likely some sort of security/government agent? Now, it seemed, although he must be in his early sixties, he was still a part of that world. And looking well on it … I hoped I'd hear more from him.

I did hear further from my mysterious American. He tracked me down and I made a visit to New York later that year. It turned out he was a key player in the US election and had a very close ear to the Presidential hopeful, whose wife was interested in astrology. The team – he said – had done some research on me, and apparently my digital profile showed connections with right wing political activity. This, they believed, was a good thing and made me even more useful to them. I explained this was all unfounded and merely conflated drivel made up by the press, and they seemed disappointed – the rest of the visit went downhill after that, and I was no longer the feted heroine and *"terrorist whisperer"* I'd started out as. I was very pleased to get home to Clenching, and back to my normal life, and didn't think much more about the US Elections and all that followed afterwards. I still get the occasional call from Melania, however. She's a Taurus by the way – stubborn to the end, and fond of her luxuries. There has to be some compensations in life, as she would see it …

Sagittarius Sun Sign cuttings

Half Man, Half Horse, All Fugitive

Coping with a Sagittarian is not hard once you learn the basic standard operating protocol – let them go. Obviously, this can be a problem if you are the governor of a high security prison but try to turn a blind eye to the toothbrush tunnelling efforts if you can. Travel is everything to Sagittarius – physical, mental, and emotional travel, and that's not easy to live or work with. If rehearsals aren't going their way, Sagittarius will (sometimes) make their excuses and exit – only to be tracked down at the airport buying a one-way ticket to somewhere else. Their sense of adventure leads them into some difficult situations, but that's the main reason for their existence – a Sagittarius life is one acted out on centre stage. All others are mere bit players in the drama.

The grass is always greener somewhere else over the rainbow with Sagittarius. Just considering the personality traits of this sign is exhausting, so please bear with me while one gather's one's celestial thoughts before transcribing. It may take some time.

Lucky Sagittarius is born with a talent for flight, and an innate fear of confinement. As the half human, half horse zodiacal representation, this is a creature who loves to undertake a difficult journey. Long distance running, endurance sports, orienteering and mountaineering are some possible outlets. Due to their inherent lack of any sense of responsibility they also excel at bail jumping and avoiding injunctions. Kind to animals, Sagittarian men make good stable hands/jockeys, but need firm tethering as they come with a high flight risk.

Jolly Astrolly! Website, 2016

Your Sagittarian Date

The planetary line-up is looking challenging for Sagittarians. No stranger to the local constabulary and feeling the impact of yet another restraining order, those born under the sign of the Centaur – half man, half steed – spend this summer planning their next great escape. Maud finds her psychic radar picking up on the word "car", and they feature heavily in the Sagittarius scope. Some Sagittarians, known for their extreme politics, love of cars and irresponsible nature may find themselves being auditioned for a TV programme. Alternatively, they could just be fulfilling the "driver" role in a contrived high-stress situation of their own making – always illegal and with scant regard for the safety of others. With that Sagittarian love of languages and necessity for overseas travel, the Centaur remains firmly in Interpol's sights this summer, as ever.

Is He Into You? website, May 2015

Holiday Sagittarius

Sagittarians are known for their interest in the animal kingdom and for being free spirits. They are unconfined by restraints of day to day living and are always jetting off somewhere without leaving a note for the milkman. Those born under this sign are great explorers, and travel widely, if not always wisely. They don't like to be organised or made to fit into a routine, which can be difficult when so many of them answer recruitment advertisements for the armed forces. However, the IQ test is the usual deciding factor at this stage of their development. Many of our "archers" enjoy holidays where mind and body are both engaged, and added to their love of animals, seek out an animal welfare project. With this in mind Sagittarius it's probably best to stick to Whipsnade, rather than North Korea.

Jolly Astrolly! Website, August 2015

ʘ

CHAPTER 12

Taurus

Hampstead, London, 2018

First, I'm not really called Sparky. My real name is Edith Vaughan, but I changed it when I got married and became Electra Haut-Dougbreah – isn't that a mouthful? It still makes me laugh sometimes. So, maybe you've not heard of me, but I'm sure you've heard of my fashion house, *Sparky*. Even if you don't know me you will almost certainly have heard my name as part of the mythical 1960s, and my rags to riches story of building a business on the kitchen table, blah blah blah, same old stuff that the media comes up with every time. I didn't want to do this – help Maud out with her memoirs. And then someone, probably my accountant, said it was time to put my side of the "Maud" story. Not an airy-fairy side as I'm sure the rest of her account is.

Maud and I have never really been pals. The differences when we were young, when this country had a very clear class structure, would have made a friendship unlikely growing up as we did. We didn't like each other anyway so it didn't matter. Her sister always preferred animals for companions and it was Quentin I had more in common with. As it turns out, there was a good reason for that. Times have changed since those days though, and our lives are linked whether she likes it or not. I'm okay with telling our story now I've thought about it, especially as I feature so much in her background. We lived under the same roof for many years as part of her household, me and my mum and our old Singer sewing machine. But you won't hear much about that part of our sorry story from Maud.

In 2018 the *Sparky* business celebrated 50 years of existence. As all the classier papers put it at the time – it was a journey from humble beginnings in the Old Rectory, in Clenching, to an A-listers' showroom in South Molton Street, London.

In fact, it was Maud's brother Quentin, a strange, "wispy" sort of boy, who first called me "*Sparky*". I wore rubber plimsolls instead of shoes when I was working in the Rectory, and I always ran everywhere. It reminded people of a character in a kid's comic of the time called Sparky, who ran so fast there were sparks coming out of his feet. I didn't really care, it meant I was saving my real shoes for "best", but my plimsolls and me entertained the young Jollybottoms at a time when entertainment was thin on the ground. We lived at the Rectory, in the attic rooms, when I was little, but somehow my poor mother managed to get us out of there and into rooms she found us in the village. Mum had started out as a cleaner for Mrs Jollybottom, Maud's grandmother, but after the old lady had died, she'd stayed on through the war and beyond. Mum took on running the place as a sort of underpaid housekeeper and nanny – but it all got to be too much, and we were better off living away from the place, and the snooty Jollybottoms.

I left school at 14 with no qualifications. It didn't matter so much then, but I could sew very well – thanks to my mum – and had a good eye for colours and styles. It was the 1960s – the best of times to be young and living and breathing fashion. The styles were changing rapidly. Living in the country it was hard to keep up with trendy looks – the only glimpses available were through magazines in the Doctors' surgery or the local hairdressers. The nearest department store selling patterns was in Gloucester town centre, and mum and I saved up desperately to buy fabric in the store if we could afford it, or off a market stall if we couldn't.

I helped mum out with cleaning at the Rectory, and with a newspaper round and a strict saving routine of putting spare ha'pennies in a jar I managed to upgrade my sewing machine and started charging money for making dresses. When the shift dresses came in during 1964, I was able to knock out three or four, sometimes six in one long day. Before then the fashion had been fitted waists and full skirts, and there was a lot of measuring and pinning – all this changed when the "in" body shape became boyish, and I suddenly acquired more customers. Quentin came in handy in those days as a real live mannequin, if his big sister Maud allowed him off the leash. We were similar in height and build, so I often got him to model for me when I was trying out one of my own designs. He stayed loyal to the company and often helped – I think of him now as the first *Sparky* house model. Of course, he wanted to be a dancer so that kept him skinny. He knew instinctively how to pose, and liked to demonstrate his ballet moves before an audience. I think the bulimia had started by accident – a childhood mishap following a yodelling demonstration. Who knew? They were always completely mad.

In 1963 I managed to get a stall on Clenching market. It was only twice a week, Fridays, and Saturdays, but I was busy the rest of the week making the clothes and fitting in casual work where I could. By now I was old enough to work in a pub, so I did a few lunchtime sessions on my days when the market was closed. The pub hours were short and very badly paid, but they fitted in with everything else I did so I was grateful for the extra couple of pounds.

Things all changed dramatically in 1966. It was the golden year when the Beatles went psychedelic, Mary Quant lipstick arrived, and England won the World Cup. I met Rupert in 1966, the chap who would start out being my mentor, then financial backer and who ended up being my husband. Although I say met, it was really meeting again as we'd known each other since village school days. Our lives though, had gone in very different ways since then.

I was closing the stall down on a Friday afternoon in February. It was dark, there was a cold wind blowing through the market and I just wanted to get home and watch *Ready, Steady, Go* with my feet up. At the end of 1965 mum and I had been given a nice council flat with a bathroom and central heating. It was luxury compared with the rented rooms we'd had before, and we were extremely grateful for the lucky break. The flat was on an estate just outside of Clenching, built on the site of an old army camp, and the only drawback was an infrequent bus service into town. I used to carry all the clothes I was selling in two old suitcases, and I can remember how they used to bruise my legs as I bumped along the road, walking on the bits not covered by the bus route. So, when Rupert suddenly appeared at my stall, asking for a closer look at one of the unsold dresses I was about to pack away, I pulled a face.

"All right, if you're quick about it but I mustn't miss my bus" I can remember saying.

I think he was a bit shocked. He wasn't used to being spoken to like that, so I explained we now lived in the sticks and relied on the bus service I couldn't miss. He turned out to be easy to talk to, and I was grateful and a bit chuffed when he gave me a lift home. On the way he offered to give me driving lessons, and I agreed, thinking to myself *"how on earth could I afford a car?"*. And he had bought the dress he'd looked at! It went to a girlfriend he had at the time, some posh bird in London called Camilla – I met her years later at a society do, and she was very complimentary about the dress, although not so nice about Rupert. It was never really a romantic thing between me and Rupert. He was down to earth despite coming from a well to do family, and we just seemed to click. We went through the motions of a love affair but looking back I realise something – they call it chemistry these days – was missing, and we just seemed to fall into a life together. We were both ambitious and prepared to work hard, although I wasn't completely sure what a lawyer's life entailed, day to day. He went out of his way to help me, someone just starting out in business and with hardly any education. He put up capital, helped me find further finance, and with his law background and family business connections together we really got *"Sparky"* off the ground. From Clenching I moved to a tiny shop in Notting Hill, just as it was becoming fashionable. When we married in early 1969 at Chelsea Town Hall it was just so exciting being a part of this creative new world. Rupert gave up his law career to concentrate more on the business. We worked well as a partnership and didn't look too closely at the nuts and bolts holding us together. *Sparky* and I, and mum, were thriving and that was all that mattered to a girl from a Gloucestershire council estate in the 1960s – it was groovy baby!

The thing in those days was to move as far away, as quickly as possible, from your real life and family. Why not make up a fairy story about yourself, if you wanted to? Nowadays we're all dissecting the past with a microscope – looking up our family tree on those TV programmes, doing DNA tests, etc. We're all desperate to find out who we are and where we've come from. They keep asking *me* to do one but I'm not sure about it, who knows what might come to light?

Anyway, along came the 1970s recession. We'd expanded quickly and suddenly raging inflation meant we couldn't keep up with the rent. When we moved from the first shop in Notting Hill I concentrated on luxury, expensive dresses – it was fabulous seeing my work worn at a film premiere, or restaurant opening. Rupert took me to art galleries in London on our rare days off – there was a medieval type of style that was really trendy at the time, so I did plenty of long, flowy type things, and they were instantly popular. Far too expensive for the average girl on the street, of course, but celebrities loved my creations; Bianca and Jerry looked fabulous in them. And they loved me, and my rags to riches fairy tale story – no-one mentioned the hard work, of course. It didn't matter, I could hold my own with any art school designer.

Except by the mid-70s the glamorous events started to dry up, and the fashion in London, especially, was becoming all about horrible punk style clothing. The public didn't want to look like Hollywood film stars in expensive garments, they preferred to look like tramps held together with safety pins. And the film stars, suddenly embarrassed by their affluence, wanted to look like the public.

We cut our losses by 1978 and closed the store. Laying off people was hard, but it didn't come as a shock to them or us. The end of my marriage did, though. Even though Rupert and I only existed as a business partnership by now, I hadn't known there was someone else waiting for him when the inevitable happened. We still had a few wealthy clients, and plenty of connections, but the cash flow had dried up and I was desperate to bring in some money. Rupert had decamped to California, by now, to live with Larry. I don't think he ever really got over the shock of the twins' birth. Sasha and Milo had been born in 1975 and even paying their nursery fees was a struggle. I was still in touch with Quentin though from the old days in Clenching, even though mum now lived in a cottage in Henley I'd bought for her.

Quentin kept me up to date with the Jollybottom news, and the more I thought about them, the angrier I became. Maud seemed to be popping up on the TV all the time now and had a regular radio slot on Radio 1 where she spouted her zodiac drivel for anyone stupid enough to listen. I remembered the unheated attic rooms in the Old Rectory, the hand me down clothes, and the sheer bloody condescension from Maud, her half-witted nymphomaniac sister, and the rest of them, all putting on their "nice" faces and keeping a firm grip on the rest of us. Apart from Quentin they were a sorry, penny-pinching bunch of hypocrites who were loathed by the locals. Too many dodgy stories of the black-market goings on in wartime had followed them down the years. I remembered stories my mum told me of being chased into the scullery by Old Man Jollybottom when he'd enjoyed himself a bit too much at some Freemasons' "do", intending to show her his "regalia". So, when I discovered one of my Hampstead neighbours was a journalist on one of the Fleet Street tabloids, I was only too happy to give him my take on Maud's caring persona. Maud's caring stopped and started with Maud, and her weirdo family, and always had done.

Of course, Quentin took some persuading to steal Maud's journals. I knew she had always kept one, so I had to be very firm with him and reminded him where his loyalties lay. I hadn't come from nothing to let myself go back there. It ended up in a bidding war between the tabloids. The headlines really went to town – "*Sixties Fashion Queen Sparky spills all on Murky Maud's family connections …*"

This was the first of two Maud events in my life that got me out of a tight spot (although if you spoke to the Jollybottoms, they'd tell you they helped me get *Sparky* launched). The second one came in 1983 when, for some unknown reason, Maud was part of the BBC coverage of the

European Song Contest in Berlin. Oddly, she was wearing one of my designs, a sparkly black and white number that had never made it on to the catwalk. I remember it well because the dress – designed during my monochrome period – somehow disappeared backstage and was never shown. We all assumed someone had pinched it, and I lost interest – even more surprising when it turned up at Eurovision on Maud! I had to admit it really looked good on her, and I couldn't have been happier when the press picked up on it. No one had the slightest interest in what the British entry was about, or their miniscule chance of winning, but when the Space Hunterz debacle took place, a picture of baffled Maud appeared in all the newspapers. Maud, wearing my dress. For once, I felt genuine gratitude towards her – funny how things turn out, isn't it?

Taurus Sun Sign Cuttings

Taurus

Saturn has been in opposition to your sign for two years but made an exit at the end of 2014. It will be popping back over the summer however to see if any progress in your wretched mess of a life has been made. This year brings finality in one form or another, so you should look upon this time as an opportunity to make a fresh start. Do not dig your heels (or hooves) in as your stubborn personality usually compels you. Instead contact any sort of decluttering organisation immediately and get on the first available programme, and let's have no more of the *"neighbours keep putting their recycling into my bin"* whining.

Jolly Astrolly! Website, April 2015

Taurus is ruled by the 2nd House – and that means money, possessions, and having the jolliest of times. More often than not they are patient and gentle creatures who love to play at the genial host. What is guaranteed to send the loveable little white bull into a stampeding beast, however, is disruption of any kind and the notion of "roughing it". This is an alien concept to a Taurus, and any managers and booking agents would do well to take heed. Venus arrives in Taurus mid-autumn 2017, with romantic promise attached. The next six months look interesting with Jupiter smiling indulgently on Taurus excesses. Don't be surprised if an enterprising individual arrives on the scene with a valuable skill – knowing how to fund those splendiferous parties would be helpful. Try listening for once, Taurus.

The Riff Magazine, September 2018

Sporty Sun Signs – Taurus

Some born under Taurus are familiar with the concept of sport but refuse to take it seriously on a personal level. As a rule, they prefer to be spectators, but if forced to participate they like a military march/square bashing session and wearing uniform. Their political aspiration is to achieve world domination in one form or another – think May Day parade in the soviet bloc era – so if it can be combined with a bit of exercise, so much the better. Ideally, two tickets for centre court are the Taurean definition of sport – watching others slog their guts out for hours on end is more or less their *raison d'etre*, as anyone employed by a Taurus will testify.

Jolly Astrolly! Website, March 2011

Press Conference following screening of "*Have you Heard, it's in the Stars*"

Hosted by: Daniel Shah, BBC, 2020

BAFTA Viewing Room 6, 195 Piccadilly,
St. James's, London W1J 9LN

The following is a transcript of the press conference reproduced here with kind permission of the Jollybottom family and their legal representatives.

Daniel Shah …

"Welcome to everyone joining us here today at BAFTA, and at home by the marvels of modern technology. We are especially honoured to have the Holy Father join us via zoom from the Vatican. Let me start by congratulating Maud and her production team on the film we have just enjoyed – "*Have You Heard, It's In The Stars*" which has already been nominated for a BAFTA Documentary award. Maud Jollybottom really needs no introduction but just to remind you she is the renowned international astrologer …"

Shah reads some biographical details from the backs of Maud's countless books.

… and finally, Maud herself describes her astrological identity as being on the Libran/Scorpion cusp with Leo rampant, which translates as witty and sociable with just a tiny hint of malevolence. So, without further ado

I'd like to open this up and have your questions for Maud – would you start by giving your name, and organisation, please?

"David Sax, Journalist, *Undacuvva Podcast*,

… would just like to add my congratulations to Maud and ask her, has she had a chance to watch the recent "*All About You*" edition featuring Electra Vaughan? Where it turns out Electra, or Sparky, as I believe Maud knows her, is actually a member of the Jollybottom family – and has the DNA test result to prove it?"

Shah whispers to Maud who looks distressed and shakes her head. He replies to Sax on Maud's behalf.

"… Maud hasn't watched this programme and doesn't understand the purpose of your question?"

David Sax

"… it turns out, according to the programme, Maud's brother Quentin and Electra are twins, born in 1947, a few years after Jericho, Maud's mother disappeared? So that would make Sparky, or Electra, Maud's half sister, wouldn't it? And Electra's mother, the late Mrs. Vaughan, would seem to be on very good terms with Maud's father, Ganglion?"

Laughter in the room

Shah asks for quiet, and whispers again with Maud

"Maud wishes it to be known she will not be making any comment on this until she has seen the programme, and will not be making any further public comment today. She asks that her family's privacy be respected. On a different note, she would like to be remembered to Mr. Sax's father, Gordon Sax, wherever he currently is. For the record Maud was a founder member, and remains an active donor of, P.L.O.P. (PRESS LANGUISHING OVERSEAS in PRISON).

Next question please, ladies and gentlemen?

"Merlin Shaughnessy, *Gelding* magazine

"… add my congratulations today but, speaking from a transgender non-binary viewpoint, does Maud agree her mother's wartime problems arose as a result of her confused sexual identity?"

Shah again speaks quietly with Maud who looks simultaneously distressed and baffled. Once again, Shah answers on her behalf.

"Maud never dwells on the past – she prefers to be thought of as a modern thinking person looking towards the future, despite being in her 80s …

Maud smiles suddenly at the crowd, and gives a small wave in the manner of the late Queen Mother

…and only asks that her mother be remembered in the way Maud and her siblings would like. For some years Mrs Jollybottom was an unofficial advisor to the *Gravity Impact Programme* at NASA. To that end Maud has made a bequest to NASA for the establishment of the *Jericho Jollybottom Research Institute into Interplanetary Flight*".

Applause

Shah waits for the applause to stop before asking for one, final question from the floor …

Mikhail Mcgillycuddy, Journalist, *New Republic* magazine

"… how does Maud feel about the persisting rumours of espionage from the Berlin days? There's talk of new information coming to light that in 1989 the superpowers …"

Daniel Shah breaks in, asking loudly for medical attention to Mr Mcgillycuddy, who is suddenly clutching his chest and unable to speak. Bright red in the face, the crowd turns to surround him as some photo-journalists rush to capture his death throes in close-up. The conference breaks up and amid all the confusion, Maud Jollybottom is gently ushered out of the room, seemingly unaware of any problem, and still smiling.

Conference Ends

Epilogue

Thank you to everyone who has followed Maud Jollybottom over the last ten years or so. She was originally created – believe it or not – as part of a "start-up" business website in 2011, initiated by me and the late Mr W. We never actually started up, but Maud continued to evolve in my imagination. Her being came about when I shamelessly "borrowed" the brilliant name of Krystal Jollybottom, a comedy character imagined by the late, great Peter Cook, progenitor of *Private Eye* and half of comedy duo Pete and Dud, amongst many other funny things. I loved the name, but Krystal wasn't quite the right moniker for the stargazing, unflinching social climber I had in mind, so her sister Maud was created and got the job, Krystal was demoted to blonde bombshell and poodle wrangler, and the rest of the Jollybottoms, of the Old Rectory, Clenching, staggered into life.

She serves no other purpose than to make you laugh. I have little knowledge of, and absolutely no training in, Astrology, and I am filled with admiration for those practitioners[1] who do put the work in and make this arcane subject accessible to the rest of us. I certainly believe there is "something in it". It will be for future generations to discover – along with many other things – what that something is.

---

[1] Anyone interested in learning further about astrology would do well by reading the books of Liz Greene, Marjorie Orr, Linda Goodman, and Shelley von Strunckel, not forgetting two excellent male astrologers (and the latter, a notable social historian) Neil Spencer and Russell Grant. If you are interested in charts and how to read them, I recommend the website Astrodienst.com as a good place to start.

*"There are more things in heaven and earth,
Horatio, than are dreamt of in your philosophy …"*

Hamlet, Act 1, Scene 5. William Shakespeare (Taurus)